# DICK

Scott Hildreth

Published by
Eralde Publishing

Cover Design Copyright © Creative Book Concepts
Text Copyright © Scott Hildreth
Formatting by Creative Book Concepts

ISBN 13: 978-0692699553

# DEDICATION

To the woman who wrapped her arms around a real-life bad boy and loved him with all her heart. Jess, this one is for you.

# PROLOGUE

**THERE** were a hundred places I would have rather been than the interrogation room of a police station, but being there wasn't the grandest of my concerns. My biggest problem was the smile I couldn't wipe from my face. The two shit-hat cops were irritating – each in their own little ways – but it was the creepy mustache that made it impossible for me to stop grinning. The night had been filled with drinking, exotic cars, a bloody umbrella, foreign diplomats, a million-dollars' worth of drugs, a Savannah Leopard, an attempted robbery, and plenty of gunfire. But, in the end, it was going to be the smile that got me into trouble.

I needed to play the part of an innocent bystander, but I was still half-drunk, which made hiding my emotions difficult. Cop number one looked like he just stepped out of a 1980's porn film, and his nasty little mustache had my face covered in a cheesy grin that made it seem like I was lying.

And, for the most part, I was.

The one with the caterpillar on his lip was wearing jeans, boots, and an untucked tee shirt. The other wore a navy-colored jacket over a light blue button-down with a loosely tied polyester tie dangling from underneath the collar. As necktie stared at me and chewed on a wooden match, Mr. Mustache paced the floor. Neither looked like any cops I had ever seen.

"We need *something*," the cop with the necktie said. "Something significant."

1

My gaze fell to his scuffed loafers. As I lifted my eyes along the length of his wiry frame, I shook my head. "You two don't even look like cops."

Cop 'stache sauntered to the edge of the table, pressed his hands to his hips, and bent at the waist slightly. "We're *detectives*," he seethed.

I shrugged and fought against the urge to smile.

He cocked an eyebrow. "I wonder if I'll look like a cop when I cuff your skinny little ass and toss you in a cell for obstruction of justice?"

I tried to pry my eyes open, but the four margaritas and three glasses of wine I had over the course of the evening made it close to impossible. I gazed at him through narrow slits. "I didn't see him that well. It was dark, and I was drunk. Hell, I'm still drunk."

It wasn't far from the truth.

He stepped away from the table and glanced at his partner. "You think she's lying, Joe? I think she's lying."

Necktie gnawed on his wooden match. "Prob'ly."

Mr. Mustache exchanged glances between us. "You know how I can tell?"

"How's that?" necktie asked.

The porn star locked eyes with me and pursed his lips. "Cause she's grinnin'."

I wasn't intimidated. Not in the least. I'd seen far too much in the last year to let two cops intimidate me. Especially when one of them looked like he should be fucking some chick with a hairy bush while *bow-chicka-wow-wow* music played in the background.

"Look," porn 'stache said. "We're just trying to put together pieces of a puzzle. We weren't there, and you were. We know you were part of it, so just tell us what happened."

2

It sounded simple, but it wasn't. Not even close. It was the most fucked up thing I had ever become a part of, and I doubted no matter how long I lived that I'd ever participate in anything half as fucked up ever again.

"I need to pee," I said.

Mustache pressed his thumbs into the pockets of his jeans. "Tell us his name, and I'll have Joe take you down to the bathroom. Hell, we might have a fresh pot of coffee."

"I've watched *Bluebloods*," I said. "If I'm not under arrest, I can leave. If I am, I can ask for an attorney to be present."

I wasn't worried about an attorney. It was my understanding one was going to show up promptly at 11:00, and I had no reason to doubt it. I was simply trying to stay awake until that time came. Whatever happened until then was going to be nothing but entertainment.

The one wearing the necktie chuckled. "Shit, Tad, we've fucked around and apprehended a *Bluebloods* trained professional. She got her a certificate of criminal justice from watching fucking T.V., maybe we should just let her go."

The porn star sat down across from me. "Just tell us what happened. And his name, we'll need a name."

The smell of cheap cologne and sweaty gym socks crept across the table and found its way into my nostrils. I shook my head, attempted to wipe the stench from my nose, and responded with a blatant lie. "I can't really remember what happened. The whole night's a big blur. Especially the part when people started shooting."

"Okay, we'll work on what he looked like later. It'll all come to you as you sober up. For now, what was his name? The one driving the Ferrari?" he asked.

I held my breath and tried to act stupid. "Fer-what?"

"The car you were in, it was a Ferrari," he said. "Well, the car you were in until he left your ass for dead."

I flattened my upper body onto the cold steel table and exhaled slowly. As the last puff of alcohol-laced breath passed my lips, I met his gaze.

His mustache stared back at me.

My mouth curled into a smirk.

"Look, sunshine. We have three-dozen eyewitnesses who saw you two in the club. I know you know what his name is and what he looks like You were with him all night. Tell us what his name is, and I'll have Joe take you to the bathroom. Then, you can have a cup of coffee and see what you can remember about everything else. How's that sound?"

I pushed my chair away from the table. "My name's Jess, not *sunshine*."

I crossed my legs, feigning lack of bladder control, and glanced at necktie. He quickly switched the match to the other side of his mouth and tossed his head toward the door. "Follow me."

"I know what *your* name is," mustache said. "I wanted *his*."

Providing his name wouldn't give them with any useful information. Half the city probably shared his first name. I glanced at the round over-sized clock hanging over the doorway.

10:30.

I still had thirty minutes. If I took my time in the bathroom and slowly sipped my coffee when we got back, I might get by with only lying to them for fifteen minutes. I could talk in circles for fifteen minutes.

"His name?" I asked over my shoulder as I followed bad cop toward the door.

4

"Yeah, I'll need that before you go."

I turned around and met his gaze. "Dick."

Mustache stood and folded his arms in front of his chest. "Excuse me?"

I studied him from head-to-toe. As our eyes locked, the corner of my mouth twisted into a smirk. "Dick."

His eyes narrowed and his jaw muscles went tense. "What'd you call me?"

"His name," I said with a shallow grin. "His name was Dick."

He chuckled, seeming slightly relieved. "Dick, huh? No last name?"

I shook my head.

"Well, when you get back, we'll need you to tell us what happened."

I laughed. "I wouldn't know where to start."

He licked the edge of his mustache with the tip of his tongue, pulling the end of it into the corner of his mouth. "At the beginning."

"The beginning?"

He nodded. "Yeah, the beginning. It's always a good place to start. Might be tough to remember all the details, I'm sure you were scared shitless with all the gunfire and commotion. Go to the bathroom, get your coffee, and we'll get started when you get back. At the beginning."

*The beginning? When I met Dick?*

*When I met him I was scared and not quite myself.*

*This? Tonight?*

*This is fucking fun.*

# ONE

## JESS

**THE** clock in my car said 3:01, but I kept it five minutes fast so I wouldn't be late to work again. Sitting in the alley roughly one hundred feet from my parking spot, the two cars stopped in front of me and the truck directly behind me caused me to wonder if the four minutes I had to spare were going to be enough. Unwilling to take the risk, I pressed my palm against the center of my steering wheel and blared the horn.

The driver of the first car got out and walked toward the black Mercedes-Benz parked in front of me. The clock clicked to 3:02.

*Fuck.*

My boss was a prick. He was the type of asshole who should have an online $99 webinar teaching the unknowing how to become assholes. I had been late enough times to know if I was late again, he would fire me on the spot, no questions asked.

I rolled down the window and pointed at the six-stall employee parking lot directly in front of the two cars blocking the alley.

I was so close.

The driver of the Mercedes opened the door and got out. He was wearing dark jeans, a powder blue untucked button-down shirt, and dress shoes. The light growth of beard that covered his face made him seem rugged and slightly more handsome than I imagined he would look without it. He clenched his fists and stretched his shoulders back, revealing an extremely broad chest.

*Dear God.*

Everything about him emanated sex.

I wagged my finger toward the empty parking stalls. "Can you pull over? I just need to get right *there!*"

He turned toward me and took a few steps. He was built like a linebacker and had the confident strut of the criminals in the books I loved to read. Mysteries and suspense were my favorites, and I always dreamed of being the girl who was the hero's main lady.

"Honk that motherfucker again and see what happens," he seethed.

*Oh wow.*

*What an asshole.*

I really needed to keep my job. I pointed beyond him and toward the bar. "I just need to park over there," I squeaked.

"Well, here in about five minutes you'll be able to."

*I've only got four.*

"Please?"

He turned away.

I cleared my throat. "Please?"

He turned around and stared. It was only for a second, but it was long enough that I realized pleading with him would probably get me nothing but an early trip to the cemetery.

He looked menacing and handsome at the same time. As much as I wanted to tell him to fuck off, his demeanor warned me against it. I raised both hands in surrender, prompting him to forget about me and approach the other driver. While they talked, I anxiously watched the two men, paying more attention to the man driving the Mercedes than the other.

They exchanged what seemed to be heated words. I turned down my music and tried to hear what was being said. Clearly frustrated, the truck parked behind me disappeared from view in my rearview mirror, speeding down the alley in reverse.

The driver of the first car was dressed like a businessman; wearing navy slacks, a dress shirt, and jacket. He shrugged and started to speak. The guy from the Mercedes shook his head and interrupted, waving his arms as he spoke. His shirt clung to the muscles of his biceps, leaving little to the imagination regarding what appeared to be a very athletic build.

"I'll give you until two weeks from Friday," the Mercedes driver said. "If you don't have it, I'll burn your house down and sell your fucking wife to the Sinaloa Cartel."

"I'll have it."

"You fucking better. I'm not fucking around, Seton. I've got that money promised out. People are counting on me, and you're making me look like a goddamned fool."

I couldn't believe what I was hearing. Visions of a drug deal gone bad or a botched kidnapping filled my mind. The driver of the first car said something in response, nodded, and got into his car.

Slightly shocked and filled with a considerable amount of curiosity, my imagination began to run wild. After a moment of gawking at the driver of the Mercedes, I closed my eyes and imagined him auctioning off the other man's wife to the highest bidder in the dirty streets of Mexico while children sold hand-made trinkets in the background.

The horn blared as my chest pressed against the steering wheel.

*Fuck.*

"Sorry," I shouted out the window.

Peering at me through the windshield of my car, his eyes narrowed to slits. "What the fuck did I tell you?"

The tone of his voice wasn't very inviting. With a mesmerizing swagger, he began walking toward me.

*Oh shit.*

As the first vehicle sped away, the muscular man stepped alongside my car.

My throat tightened.

He leaned down and peered through the open window. "What the fuck with you and the fucking horn?"

I shrugged and fought to swallow the lump that worked its way up my throat.

His eyes surveyed the interior of the car and eventually met mine. "God damn, you're a cute little bitch."

Most who knew me described me as feisty or mouthy. No one had ever referred to me as a *bitch* and walked away without me giving them a piece of my mind. I pressed my tongue to the roof of my mouth, parted my dry lips, and prepared to speak.

"Thank you," I murmured.

Intimidated, a little scared, and completely oblivious to what time it was, I broke his gaze and glanced at the clock.

3:07.

*Fuck.*

I inhaled a slow shallow breath. A faint hint of his cologne caused my mouth to salivate.

He stepped away from the car and tossed his head to the side. "Get out."

"I uhhm. I'm late for…"

"Get out."

The tone of his voice was confident, but not cocky. He wasn't asking me; he was telling me, but for some reason I felt like it was my choice. My eyes fell to his waist. A very noticeable bulge in his jeans caused me to do two things:

Swallow heavily.

And open my car door.

Dressed in my normal work attire of Chuck's, jean shorts, and a tee shirt, I nervously stood no more than five feet in front of him. He folded his arms in front of his chest and studied me carefully from head-to-toe. Prying my eyes from his prominently chiseled facial features was almost impossible.

Almost.

I gazed beyond him and focused on the back of his car.

His hand lightly grazed against my cheek. He pressed against my chin with his thumb, turning my head until our eyes met. "What's your name?"

I nervously gazed back at him, trying not to seem scared. For some reason, I wasn't, and I couldn't for the life of me understand why. His finger traced along the outline of my jaw.

My legs went weak.

"I'm going to be fired," I murmured.

"Your name," he said. "I asked you what your name was."

"Jess." I tilted my head to the side, pulling it away from his hand. "I'm Jess."

He coughed out a light laugh. "You pull away because you're scared? Or you just want me to think you're hard to get?"

11

His questions caught me off guard. "I uhhm, I was just…"

He cocked his head to the side and his mouth curled into a mischievous little grin. "Doesn't really matter."

"What doesn't matter?"

"The reason you pulled away. It doesn't matter."

My eyes fell to the street. I studied the tips of his shiny black shoes and felt guilty for wanting him to touch me again. If anyone else would have touched me the way he did, I would have slapped them. But, I hadn't had sex in forever. And he was *really* hot.

"Why?" I asked. "Why doesn't it matter?"

He reached for my chin and lifted against it until our eyes met. "Because it doesn't." He released my chin and lowered his hand.

My eyes followed his hand as he reached into his pocket and removed his wallet. He produced a business card and flipped it between his fingers with the finesse of a magician performing card tricks.

He extended his hand. "Here."

As I reached for the card my eyes once again fell to his very noticeable bulge.

I took the card from his hand. My mouth went dry, and responding in any manner that included speaking was quickly excluded as an option. I fought to swallow, slowly raised my shoulders, and simply shrugged.

"Call me, text me, whatever. Don't make me wait long." He shook his head. "Jesus. Looking at you makes me…"

I wanted him to finish his thought, but he never did.

I fought against the tightness in my throat. There were a million things I felt I should have said, and half as many again that I wanted to, but for whatever reason, none of them came out. I wondered if he felt my silence was an invitation or maybe acceptance of his request to call him.

I tried to force myself to say something, but instead lowered my eyes until they met the outline the rim of his cock made against the leg of his jeans.

*Holy shit!*

He reached for his back pocket. "You work in the bar?"

I swallowed a mouthful of saliva and nodded.

"Patel's an asshole."

I exhaled and nodded again, shocked that he knew the owner of the bar by name. "Uh huh."

As he shoved his wallet into the back pocket of his jeans, the tail of his shirt raised slightly, but it was enough for me to see what it had been concealing.

A pistol was wedged between the waist of his jeans and his hip. I tore my eyes away from the gun, hoping he didn't notice me staring.

Without speaking, he turned away.

"Call me," he said over his shoulder as he opened his car door.

I stood and stared.

"I mean it," he said. "If you don't, I'll hunt your little ass down, Jess."

*And what? Burn my fucking house down?*

I raised the shiny black card in the air and waved it in his direction as if agreeing to his demand. As his car sped away, I glanced down at the what he had handed me. A telephone number and his first name was all that was printed on the card.

I gazed down at his name and grinned.

*Dick.*

How appropriate.

# TWO

# DICK

**BEING** around Seton made me think of kidnapping his wife. Thoughts of his wife made me daydream of bitches with round asses, and the mental image of that brought me right back to the girl from the bar.

Jess.

Her ass was shaped like a "C", and I could easily imagine it bent over in front of me while I shoved her full of dick. Right in the middle of trying to scare my $100,000 payment out of Seton, however, wasn't the best time for me to be losing focus. In a last ditch effort to clear my mind of such thoughts, I pressed the tip of my index finger against the skin immediately underneath my right eye and pulled it down as far as I felt I could.

With my eye bulging, I turned toward Seton. "Look in this motherfucker, would you?"

He shook his head in an apparent attempt to get me to leave him alone. "Dick, I was just…"

"God damn it, I'm fucking serious," I hissed.

Using my free hand, I lifted my eyelid with the tip of my finger as I continued to pull down on the skin beneath my eye with my other hand. "Take a look in this motherfucker."

With reluctance, he tilted his head back and peered into my eye.

15

"What am I looking for?"

"Compassion, kindness, hell, I don't know. Maybe a little sympathy. You see a sympathetic person in there? Or a fleck of kindness?"

He stared into it as if searching for something of significance.

"You see any of that shit in there?" I asked.

He sighed heavily. "I don't think so."

"Take a good look, god damn it. I want you to be sure. Even a glimmer?"

"I don't…"

"God damn it, Seton. Take a good fucking look," I said through my teeth. "Look deep. I want you to be sure. Even a hint? You see a fucking hint of concern in there?"

He leaned away. "I uhhm. I uhhm, I don't think so."

I closed my eye and rubbed my fingertip against the eyelid. As I glared at him with my other eye, I shook my head. "You know why?"

He shrugged.

"Because I don't give a fuck," I growled. "I'm an emotionless businessman. And a prick."

I blinked a few times. "This is a business, and I'm a fucking businessman. If you fail, the system fails. If the system fails, I fail."

I needed the $100,000 he owed me. I already had it committed, and if he didn't follow through, people were going to be disappointed with me.

Extremely disappointed.

I motioned around my living room with both hands. "Look around you."

He glanced around the room nervously.

Decorated with lavish furniture and artwork worth more than he'd earn in a lifetime, the interior of the home reeked of wealth.

"Do I look like a fucking failure?"

He shook his head.

"You know why?"

He shrugged. "Because you're not?"

"Because I'm fucking not," I said with a nod.

I cleared my throat. "I wasn't joking about your wife, Seton. She's a pretty fucker, and with those new tits you bought her right after Christmas last year, those Mexicans would go crazy to get a shot at her. They love blondes, you know. Did you know that? About the blondes?"

I watched his Adam's apple rise and fall. "I uhhm. I'll get it to you."

I walked to the couch and sat down. As he nervously studied me, I crossed my legs and continued. "I know you will. You know how I know it?"

He shook his head.

"Because if you try really hard you can imagine your wife down in Juarez sucking some fat Mexican's sweaty cock while he's eating a plate of chili rellenos. And my guess is that you don't like the thought of it one fucking bit."

His face filled with anger and quickly washed to one of concern.

"Hell of a thing, thinking that some Mexican traded a box of grapefruit for your wife, isn't it? That's what I'd trade her for, Seton. Just to teach you a lesson about fucking with my money. I'd trade her for grapefruit." I chuckled. "Well, that and maybe a couple of those avocados they grow down there."

His face was ruby red and sweat quickly began to form on his brow.

I nodded as I glanced around the room. "I'd swap that bitch for a box of grapefruit and half a dozen avocados. You ever had those Mexican avocados? Hass, that's what they call 'em. *Hass*. They're good as fuck."

"I said I'll have it. I'll have it."

The business I was in prevented me from being a compassionate man. "I asked you a fucking question, Seton. The avocados. You ever have 'em? They've got a little sticker on 'em that says 'Hass'."

He shook his head.

"You should try 'em. They're fucking good."

I kept my eyes locked on his until he broke my gaze. As he looked away I glanced at my watch.

"God damn it, now you've fucked around and damned near made me late." I jumped up from the couch. "Go get my fucking money and don't come back until you've got it. If you're not back here by two weeks from Friday, I'm going to trade your wife for a box of fucking fruit."

Sadly, if he didn't pay me, I would do just that. I'd spend fifty grand hiring someone to kidnap his wife and haul her ass to Mexico. After she was safely in the country, I'd drive down, meet with the Sinaloa Cartel, and trade the bitch for a box of fucking grapefruit. I'd probably have someone make a video of the transaction, just to convince others not to fuck with my money.

I motioned toward the door. "Let yourself out. I've got to change clothes."

As I heard the front door open, I shouted over my shoulder. "Two weeks, motherfucker!"

I quickly changed clothes, grabbed $5,000 from the safe, and ran to the garage. As I pulled out of the driveway, I mentally prepared my schedule for the evening. Basically, I had one thing I *had* to do.

Pay for a leopard.

It had been two days since I met Jess in the alley, and I hadn't heard from her yet. I decided after I dropped off the money I would stop by the bar and see if she lost her job or somehow convinced Patel to let her keep it.

Either way, I'd find her.

I merged onto the highway, pressed down on the gas, and maneuvered around the traffic until I reached an open stretch of road. After setting the speed control, my mind faded to thoughts of Jess' round ass.

I pressed my thumb against the button on the steering wheel, activating the phone.

"Call. The Brisco."

After the third ring, the phone was answered. *"The Brisco."*

"Hey, this is Dick. I need to make a reservation."

*"Good afternoon, Dick. How many will be in your party?"*

"Two," I said.

*"And what time works for you?"*

It was Wednesday night. Patel's bar wouldn't have fifteen people in it even if it was busy.

"Nine o'clock," I said.

*"Party of two for nine. Anything else I can do for you?"*

"Table in the back? In the corner by the fireplace?"

*"Consider it done."*

"Appreciate it."

*"See you at nine, Dick."*

I pressed the button and ended the call.

The look on Jess' face when I handed her my business card told me convincing her to go to dinner would be a pretty simple task. The look in her eyes told me she was going to be an adventurous little bitch.

19

## DICK

And the eyes never lie.

# THREE

# JESS

**WORKING** for a living sucked big fat dicks. Deep within me, a little rich girl resided, all I lacked was the resources.

The Benjamins. Moolah. Bank. Dat swag money.

And my job as a waitress at the shitty little bar I worked at wasn't getting me any closer.

"Hey, this tastes like shit." A voice beside me shouted.

I glanced over my left shoulder. A middle-aged man with a sweet as fuck comb-over raised his half-finished glass of beer in the air.

"It's a beer. What'd you expect? I'll bring you shot of vodka to pour in it. It might help."

He looked confused. Maybe he hoped to get more from me, I don't know. But if he expected me to make a glass of beer taste good, he was going to be in for a really long fucking night.

He shot me a glare. "Huh?"

"It's beer. Beer taste like shit. What do you want me to do?"

He shrugged. "Get me something different?"

"Something that tastes good? Like an Alice in Wonderland or a White Russian? Or some of our fifty-cent wings? They taste good. Actually, they're good as fuck. They're dry rubbed, not battered and fried like everyone else's. Oh, and the Black and Blue Burger. It's good."

21

He chuckled a light laugh. At least he found humor in my sarcastic attitude. He raised the glass as if offering it to me and shook his head. "How about a Budweiser?"

It seemed like a ridiculous resolution. "Budweiser's beer, so it'll taste like shit, too. It'll be like comparing a cat turd to a dog turd. They're both turds."

I thought I was quick-witted. Funny. Cute.

He looked unamused. "Just smell this. Really. Something's wrong with it."

I knew what was wrong with it, it was a glass of stinking fucking beer. For entertainment value alone, I turned around, snatched the glass from his hand, and took a whiff.

My stomach convulsed. I fought not to puke. "Jesus. Fuck." I shook my head and tried to clear the smell from my nostrils. It didn't help.

I stared at the glass of beer. It *seemed* normal. "What was this nasty fucker?"

"Shock Top."

I couldn't believe he'd choked down half of it. I raised my shoulders and the glass in apology. "Sorry. I'll get you a Bud."

He smiled and nodded his head in appreciation.

The bar I worked in catered to everyone from the owner's drug-dealing friends to the lower layer of the city's upper crust. As a result of waiting on the eclectic group of patrons, I was intimidated by no one, and felt that I was able to always be myself. Instead of kissing my customer's asses for a tip, I provided great service and a smart mouth.

I was the same person for everyone, always. Eventually, most grew to like me. Those who didn't just had to learn to live with my attitude, foul mouth, and sharp wit until they were done with their drink or meal.

I carried the glass of liquid filth up to the bar. "The Shock Top's fucked up. Smells like ass."

Gabe spun around. "Bad?"

"Smell it." I handed him the glass.

He raised the glass to his nose. His eyes went into full squint and his mouth puckered. "Holy shit!"

"Yeah."

He stared at me like it was my fault. "What the fuck?"

"Dunno. Don't care. Pour me a Bud for table nine. Guy drank half a glass of that shit. I'm gonna comp the table. Actually, give me three Buds."

"Got it."

I peered over the bar. Katie looked like she was waving an F-16 onto an aircraft carrier. I glanced over my shoulder, saw no one, then pointed to myself.

She nodded. "Hey Jess. Guy at seventeen asked for you by name."

I grinned. "Me?"

"You're the only Jess."

"Sweet. Thanks."

I dropped off the three beers. "Sorry about all that. Your food and the beers are on the house. Here's one for each of you."

Comb over raised his glass, as did his two friends. I smiled in return. "Again, I'm sorry. Next time you come in, ask for me. Name's Jess."

"Thanks, Jess."

I smiled and turned around. Wednesday night wasn't a busy night for us at the bar, so adding another table was exciting. I maneuvered through the empty tables toward the booth that requested me by name. Maybe I could pay my rent *and* afford to eat if things kept improving –

and no one ordered the Shock Top.

"What can I--"

*Oh shit.*

It was *him.*

Dick.

I swallowed hard. "--get for you."

He folded his arms in front of his chest and leaned against the wall. "What time do you get off?"

I cocked my hip. "Excuse me?"

"Work." His eyes slowly took in every inch of my five foot four frame. Twice. "What time do you get off?"

I felt like he'd slowly fucked me. Without permission. "You come in to hit on me, or to order?"

He shrugged. "Both."

I pursed my lips and tried to act unimpressed. "What can I get you?"

"Six wings, all legs. Two shots of Gran Patron. The Platinum. And a couple of limes."

I nodded. "That it?"

His eyes were still locked on mine. "For now."

Breaking his gaze wasn't easy. Not at all. His eyes were a strange color of the lightest blue, and as much of an intimidating prick as he was, his eyes told a different story. They were inviting.

I wanted to let him know I wasn't the scared little girl who he had met in the alley a few days prior. I was independent, adventurous, intelligent, and had more self-esteem than any other girl I knew.

As much as I didn't want to, I turned away. "I'll be back."

Normally, I worked the 3:00 to 11:00 shift, and left a little after eleven. Some nights I stayed later if we were busy, but it was infrequent.

24

I had no idea what Dick wanted from me, but I had thought about him several times since the day I met him, I just wasn't willing to call him. I wasn't *that* girl.

Katie worked the 11:00 to 7:00 shift, and was preparing to tip out the bartender.

"You get seventeen?" she asked.

I leaned against the bar. "Yeah."

I pressed my finger against the screen and placed Dick's order. "Hey, would you pick up my tables if I left early?"

She looked up from her stack of tips. "You were just bitching about rent. You're gonna leave early?"

"Maybe."

"Seventeen? He's cute."

"Maybe."

She glared. "Maybe he's cute?"

"He's *something*. I met him on Monday. In the alley. He was blocking the drive and I honked at him."

She went back to counting. "Yeah, I'll pick it up if you want."

"I'll let you know in a minute," I said.

I grabbed the two shots of Patron and walked past Comb over's table. "You guys doing alright?

He glanced over his shoulder. "Great."

I glanced at my other table; a man and a woman who appeared to be on an awkward Craigslist date. They sat across from each other talking, still nursing their first glasses of wine. I turned toward the corner and halfway to his table realized I'd forgotten the limes.

*Fuck.*

He was talking on the phone when I got to the booth. I carefully placed the two shots on the edge of the table, and before he had a chance to say anything, spoke.

"Be right back with the limes," I whispered.

He pulled the phone away from his ear, motioned toward it with his eyes, and grinned. I walked to the bar and got the limes, wondering why he seemed so much different than he did the day we met.

Maybe he burned the guys house down or sold his wife to the cartel, and now he was in a better mood. Maybe the guy paid his debt, and Dick didn't have to do those things. In my experiences, how we react to the worst life has to offer us defines who we truly are.

My guess was the Dick sitting in the booth was a shallow lie, and the Dick in the alley was the real Dick.

The real Dick was a real dick.

I slid the lime-filled shot glass between the two glasses of tequila and sat down across from him. "Here you go."

He pushed one of the shot glasses toward me. "Here."

I glanced at the glass. "Here what?"

"Drink with me."

I pushed it toward him. "I'm working. I'll get fired."

He chuckled and pushed it back. "Surprised that didn't happen on Monday."

"Patel wasn't here."

He offered a shrug as an advance apology. "If I drink both of these, I'm going to be half-drunk and it's anyone's guess how I'll be acting when we go to dinner later. If I had to guess?" I'd guess I'll be all over your cute little ass. But, if you drink one of 'em, I'll be on my best behavior. I promise. So, either drink one, or not."

I acted unaffected by his sexual innuendo. "Oh, we're going to

26

dinner, huh? I didn't hear you ask."

"I've got a reservation at 9:00. For two."

I glanced at the tequila. I wanted him to drink them both and see how he'd act, but I felt like I needed one – if not both – before I agreed to go to dinner. "So, what, you're just driving around asking women if they'll go with you until you find someone dumb enough to agree?"

He picked up a lime and bit into it. His mouth puckered and he shook his head. "Jesus. You're a mouthy little bitch. Are you the same girl I met the other day?"

I watched him threaten a man's life over an unpaid debt. He had a gun, a laser sharp glare, an attitude, and a really big dick. In the alley, he was intimidating. Now, sitting across from me, he wasn't. His eyes met mine. I felt weak.

In a good way.

"I was tired. I'd been up late and hadn't eaten. I was off my game," I lied. "So, you just stopped in to ask me to dinner?"

He sniffed the lime. "I couldn't get you or your cute little ass off my mind. So, I made the reservation for *us*. You and me."

I lifted my eyes from the tequila. My mouth was salivating. I met his gaze. "Before you asked me?"

He nodded. "I didn't need to ask. I could see it in your eyes."

"Arrogant much?"

He raised his eyebrows in acknowledgement of my sarcastic remark, then studied me as he sucked on the lime. "You're sure a mouthy little bitch. And I'm not arrogant. I'm astute."

I already decided. I was going. I wanted to know more about him. How, at less than 30 years old he was driving a new Mercedes-Benz.

And why he carried a gun.

Somewhere between conversations about guns, money, and Wednesday night dinner dates, maybe we could discuss the bulge in his jeans.

"Where?" I asked.

I really didn't care. He could have said Burger King, and I would have agreed.

He slumped in his seat slightly, studied me, and shook his head as if he couldn't believe his eyes.

I liked it.

A lot.

"The Brisco," he said.

*Fuck. Fuck. Fuck.*

The Brisco was an upscale restaurant that charged $200 a plate for dinner, and $20 for a drink. I wasn't dressed for the occasion. Hell, I *couldn't* dress for the occasion.

"I can't go wearing this, and my roommate is banging her college quarterback boyfriend and I can't go home until midnight." I shrugged. "So changing is out of question."

I didn't have a roommate, but it sounded good. It was my way out of his dinner offer without telling him I didn't own anything that The Brisco would allow me to wear.

He lifted one of the shot glasses and sniffed it. "No shit? Who's he play for?"

"Former. He's out now. Works as a bouncer."

"Where?"

"I don't know. I'm not dating him, she is." I stood up and pointed to my shorts. "But I can't wear this. Thanks, though."

"Forget your lame assed excuses, you're going. The mall closes at

10:00. I'll buy a dress."

*You're gonna buy me a dress?*

"You're gonna buy me a dress?"

"I'm going to take you to dinner. The dress is part of it."

"Are you serious?"

"About which part? That I can't get you and your cute little ass off my mind, or the part about buying the dress?"

"Uhhm." I shrugged. "Both."

"Turn around."

"What?"

"Turn around. You know what that means, right? Like spin in a circle real slow. Turn around."

"I'm not turning around."

He cocked an eyebrow and stared. It was the same stare he gave me when I honked the horn. My face felt hot and tingly. My pussy soon followed. I lasted all of three seconds.

Slowly, I turned around.

He scratched the side of his head. "Yeah."

"Yeah what?"

"Jesus. You asked me if I was serious. I said 'about what, the ass or the dress?' You said 'both.' I said 'turn around.' You did. I said 'Yeah.' Yeah, Jess. I'm serious. About your ass. And about the dress." He pushed the tequila a little closer to me. "Now, drink your fucking shot."

He was wearing a black button-down shirt, dark wash jeans, and rocking a slight growth of beard. He looked good. *Really good.* The thought of it all excited me. I loved spur of the moment shopping, hot guys, fancy restaurants, and Mercedes Benz's. I just couldn't afford any of them.

I nodded. "If you'll buy me a dress, I'll go get someone to cover my shift."

He rolled his eyes and tilted his head toward the tequila. I picked up the shot on my side of the table, downed it, and reached for his.

His eyes filled with wonder, and his face with disbelief. I lifted the other shot and downed it. The corner of his mouth curled up slightly. I grabbed one of the limes and bit into it.

I turned toward him and winked. "Pull your car around to the back door."

He sat up in his seat and grinned. As he slid out of the booth, his biceps flared through his shirt. "Bring me my tab."

*God damn, you're sexy.*

"Dinner's on you. Patron's on me."

He slid out of the booth and stood. "I'll pull around."

There were a few things I didn't have any business doing.

One of them was drinking tequila.

The other was being in the presence of a criminal.

But only one was a stipulation of my probation.

# FOUR

# DICK

**WE** sat at a table in the rear of the restaurant. Wearing her new sleeveless black dress, Jess looked like she stepped right out of an ad in a women's magazine. I couldn't decide if her brown hair had blonde highlights or if her blonde hair had brown highlights. It seemed like a perfect 50/50 mixture of both. Her brown eyes weren't dark like most that I'd seen, they were more of a translucent color.

Almost a burnt orange.

She talked fast and used her hands to gesture a lot, which made her a very entertaining person to listen to – and to watch. It was easy to get lost in just watching her be herself. The day we met in the alley I planned to fuck her and forget her, but now that I had spent the majority of the night with her, I was enjoying her company more than anyone else I had spent time with since I got out of prison. I still wanted to fuck her, but forgetting her was something I was afraid might not happen.

Ever.

As much as I knew I may never forget her, allowing her to be in my life on a regular basis wasn't an option. For me, a woman was a risk, a huge risk. And I wasn't in the risk taking business.

I was a criminal and an asshole.

And I was good at being both.

She lowered her wine glass and cocked her head slightly. "So what is it that do you do exactly?"

We had finished eating, and I wanted to talk about sex, outsmarting the law, or the arrival of my new leopard, but not what I did for money. I decided to play along. Sort of. "The truth or a lie?"

She took another sip of wine. "Truth."

I didn't tell anyone the truth. "Entrepreneur," I said, stretching the truth to its outer limits.

In my thirty years on earth, I'd fucked more women than Wilt Chamberlain, been to juvenile detention twice, prison once, and arrested more times than I could count. My current occupation – by definition – was a combination of a criminal and a vigilante of sorts, but I liked to call myself an entrepreneur.

It just sounded better.

She slid her glass of wine to the side. "Bullshit."

It was bullshit, but I couldn't really tell her the truth. Admitting the truth to anyone about what I did would be a foolish move on my part.

Very foolish.

"Why do you say it's bullshit? I'm an entrepreneur."

"You threatened to kill that guy in the alley. You said you were going to burn down his house and sell his wife to the drug cartel. Normal people don't say stuff like that."

I couldn't believe she caught all of that while she was sitting behind me in her car. Either she had hypersensitive hearing, or I talked too damned loud.

"I'm not normal people. I'm uhhm. I'm what you'd call…"

I struggled with what to say. I wasn't a normal person, I didn't act like a normal person, and I couldn't claim to be a normal person. While I attempted to formulate a variation of the truth – or a really well thought out lie – she leaned forward and pried her way into my line of sight.

"A criminal," she said.

"Whoa. What the fuck? Why would you say that?"

"In the alley. You had a gun."

*Perceptive little bitch.*

"So."

"It's simple mathematics," she said. "One, you carried a gun. And it was shoved in your pants. Two, you threatened that guy's life. And three, you told him if he didn't pay you, you'd sell his wife to the cartel."

She relaxed into her seat as if she'd made her point. As she reached for her wine, she raised her index finger and blurted out yet another reason. "And four, you drive a Mercedes."

I chuckled. "Driving a Benz isn't a crime."

"You're not old enough to drive a car like that."

I found the last statement funny. The rest of it, not so much. I responded to the latter. "I sure as fuck am."

"No you're not."

"I'm not going to argue with you. That car's paid for, and I'm the one who bought it. So, obviously I'm old enough."

She cocked and eyebrow. "What'd it cost?"

"I don't remember. Hundred and something."

Her eyes went wide. "A hundred and something grand? And you paid for it? Like *paid* for it?"

"Yeah. I bought the fucker. I think it was $128,000."

"I want to do whatever it is you do. It'd take…" She took a drink of wine and gazed beyond me for a moment. After a long minute of thinking, she looked at me again. "A little more than fifty years to buy one."

I choked on my scotch. "Fifty years?"

"Yeah. I make about forty or fifty bucks a week I could call *extra*. You know, what I spend on clothes and stuff. So, fifty bucks a week, fifty-two weeks a year, that's $2,600 a year extra. Fifty years of that would be $130,000."

I was impressed. And shocked. "Jesus. You're good at math. But what the fuck? Fifty bucks extra a week? That's fucking ridiculous."

She wagged her eyebrows. "Welcome to my life."

I tried to get a grasp on living with fifty extra bucks a week. It didn't make sense to me. Since I was sixteen, I'd hustled for everything I made. My hustling got me in some serious trouble, but it was also very rewarding.

And fun.

To think I knew someone who worked for a living and made fifty extra bucks a week was incomprehensible to me. I wanted to save her from her ridiculous job and the agony I was sure she was forced to live with, but knew better than to make an attempt.

Stuffing her full of cock and then sending her mouthy little ass home to her roommate and the football player was more like it. I decided to start a new line of questioning. Sort of. "What are you good at?"

"I'm good at a lot of things, but I thought we were talking about you?"

I cleared my throat. "We *were*. You bitched about my car, and then you said you made fifty bucks a week extra. Now we're talking about you and how you're not making any money at Patel's bar. Maybe you need to slow down on the wine so you can keep up with the convo."

"I'm not drunk, I'm just feeling good."

I liked watching her lips move. She had an amazing mouth. "Open your mouth."

"What?"

"Your mouth, open it."

She scrunched her nose. "Why?"

I glared at her. After a few seconds of nervously squirming around in her seat, she turned to face me and opened her mouth. I didn't want to look in her mouth, I just wanted her to do what I told her to. I folded my arms in front of my chest and imagined feeding her my dick, one thick inch at a time.

"Alright," I said. "I've seen enough."

She closed her mouth and licked her lips. "What was that about?"

I shrugged and took a sip of scotch.

She extended her index finger. "I'm not so drunk that I can't see what it is you're doing. You're changing the subject, criminal."

It seemed strange to be on the receiving end of harassment, especially at the hands of a woman. I tossed my hands in the air in an exaggerated – but playful – fashion. "We don't have a subject. You were just showing me how wide you could open your pretty little mouth. Now I've got your mouth *and* that cute little ass of yours to think about."

She huffed out a heavy sigh. One would have thought I spent the entire evening discussing sex. Truth be told, I hadn't even started.

She raised her glass of wine and immediately realized it was empty. "Yeah. Okay, so you gave me your little business card in the alley. And then you hunted me down, just like you said. Now you're making me open my mouth. What do you want from me?"

"Spend some time with you. Get to know you." I took a short sip of my scotch and shrugged. "See what happens."

35

"See what happens?" She leaned forward and stared straight into my eyes. "That's code for *see if I can fuck this bitch*."

I choked on my scotch. Again. I normally didn't keep track of such things, but it was the third time. And it was scotch. It burned. Bad.

"Son-of-a-bitch." I was pissed, but couldn't help but laugh. "You've got to stop making me do that."

She raised her empty wine glass. "I wish I had something to choke on."

I fought against the urge to smile, but didn't totally succeed.

"What?" she snapped.

"You want something to choke on? I can resolve that problem. Quick."

"Here we go again. I was talking about my empty wine glass, and you're thinking about sticking your big fat dick in my mouth. I don't know about you, *Dick*."

"Big fat dick? What do you know about my dick?"

She studied me for a few long seconds, and then reached into her purse. "Nothing. Forget I said anything. I'm drunk. Well, not drunk. Just drunk-ish."

She spread lip gloss on her lips, smacked them together a few times, and dropped the tube into her purse. "If it makes you feel any better, I'm a criminal too."

"Excuse me?"

She pointed to herself and nodded. "A criminal. I've been arrested."

"I can't wait to hear this. For what? Being a mouthy bitch?"

"Kicking a cop in the nuts."

It didn't surprise me. "Seriously? A real cop or a Wal-Mart cop?"

"Real cop. Real cop car. Real jail cell. Real judge. Real jury. Real everything. The fucker pulled me over for speeding, and was going to write me a ticket for not having proof of insurance. I had proof of insurance, but he wouldn't accept it."

"So you kicked him in the nuts?"

"No. I kicked him in the nuts because he grabbed me."

"Why'd he grab you?"

"Because he told me to stop and I didn't."

"Stop what?"

"Walking away while he was talking to me."

"So you kicked him in the nuts?"

"Yep. Twice. I just paid my insurance premium, and had the proof on my phone. I opened the proof of insurance, you know, the .pdf document the insurance company sent me. So I got it and showed him my phone and said 'here's the proof.' And he said 'that's not proof, I need a printed copy.' And I said 'no you don't, you *want* a printed copy. You need proof. You have proof.'

And I turned around and started walking back to my car. So, he grabbed my arm and spun me around. Fucker starts screaming about how I need to do what he says and all kinds of crazy shit. I would have been fine with all that, but he wouldn't let go of my arm. I told him to let go. He didn't. So, I kicked him in the nuts.

Twice.

Fucker arrested me, and charged me with assault on a law enforcement officer. Now I'm on probation. So, you're not the only criminal at the table."

I wasn't going to let her goad me into admitting I was a criminal. I shot her a grin to acknowledge her accomplishment.

She grinned in return. "So, back to what we were talking about.

What do you want from me, *Dick*?"

I glared at her. "Will you stop saying my name like that?"

"I will if you tell me what you want."

"I haven't decided yet. I've got a few ideas, though."

She made eye contact, leaned over the center of the table, and grabbed my glass of scotch. After two sips, she winced, coughed, and wiped her mouth. "Bullshit. I wish once, just once, that a guy would be truthful. I ask you what you do, and you say you're an entrepreneur. I ask you what you want, and you say you haven't decided. Every guy I ever dated ended up being a liar. Be different, *Dick*. Tell the truth."

I grabbed my scotch out of her hand and drank what was left in the glass. I had nothing to lose in telling her the truth. Not really. I inhaled a deep breath, studied her for a moment and decided *what the fuck*. "When I met you in the alley, I thought you were a cute little bitch, just like I told you. In fact, the more I looked at you, the cuter you got. You made my dick stiff, Jess. All ten inches of it."

Her eyes went wide. Real wide.

My mouth twisted into a smirk. "Yeah. I said ten. And it's about as fat as your skinny little wrist. I made you open your mouth just because, but when you did, I imagined watching every fucking inch of it sliding past those pouty little lips of yours. You know the lips I'm talking about right? The ones you just spread that lip butter on a minute ago?"

She stared back at me with her mouth agape.

I stood up, opened my wallet, and tossed $500 on the table. "Get up."

Her brown eyes met mine. "Huh?"

I tossed my head toward her purse. "Get up. Grab your purse. We're leaving."

She stood up. "Where are we going?"

"Back to my place. I'm tired of arguing with you. I'll just show you what I want."

"What if I don't want to do what you want to do?"

"You do. You're just too busy running your fucking mouth to realize it." I coughed out a laugh. "But here pretty soon it'll be too full for you to talk."

# FIVE

# JESS

**HE** was an absolute asshole. I liked assholes, but I doubted that was the only thing about him I liked. After struggling with it for some time, I decided it was his confidence. It seemed he couldn't contain it. And, I liked that about him. His walk. His attitude. His demands.

He had a big dick and he knew it.

His home was unlike anything I'd ever seen, and his garage was bigger than my entire house. Filled with exotic cars, motorcycles, and jet-skis, it was further proof that he was involved in something other than a common job for common wages.

I found that to be strangely attractive as well.

It was crazy thinking I agreed to a one-night stand with him, but I did. It was something I never would have guessed I'd do willingly, and in fact, I prided myself in never having a one-night stand by agreement or otherwise.

After I agreed, I immediately regretted it, but the regret didn't last long.

As soon as he took off his pants, it vanished.

He unbuckled his belt. "So you understand what this is, right?"

"Yep."

I was half-drunk, horny, and ready to be his fuck puppet. My eyes fell to his waist. I desperately wanted to see it. I was ready. He pushed his jeans past the base of his cock, taking his boxers with them at the same time. When the waistband cleared the tip, I gasped.

*Holy shit.*

His cock looked like the rest of him. Oversized. Thick. Muscular. Prepared for action. I stared. Seconds later, I realized I was still gawking at it with my mouth wide open. I probably looked like an overanxious sex-starved idiot.

All of which were true, but I didn't want him to know.

"Bend over the bed," he said.

I looked up. He was shirtless.

*Dear. Fucking. God.*

I would have done a fucking cartwheel and a backflip if he'd told me to. Thankfully, he hadn't. At least not yet.

His muscles were covered in more muscles. His ripped abdomen and broad chest defined sexy. I eagerly pushed my panties to the floor and bent over the bed. I felt my dress clear my ass and bunch up around my waist. I bit into my lower lip and prepared for him to fill me with his ten inches of thickness.

I felt his warm breath against my wet mound.

I'd never had a guy go down on me without begging him to, and even then it rarely happened. There always seemed to be an excuse supporting why it either didn't need to happen, or couldn't happen.

Dick needed no invitation.

Without warning, his tongue licked along my slit perfectly and with precision. I twisted my hips, buried my face into the comforter, and released a sigh of pleasure. Not since Bobby Buckley finger banged me for the first time underneath the bleachers in middle school had anything felt so good.

His tongue circled my clit. He sucked, nibbled, and fingered his way into my pussy and into my heart. Fully prepared for a one-night stand, but in no way ready for him to eat my pussy, my heart went aflutter.

His fingers worked in and out while his mouth sucked on my clit. His tongue flicked against my little swollen nub with each stroke of his finger, and together, they quickly brought me into a drunken state of ecstasy.

While he continued to suck and lick, I floated away, into a place I hadn't yet known. The excitement of it all – his bad boy attitude, his dick-ish behavior, and his wealth – proved to be just too much.

I wailed out in pleasure as my body convulsed, reaching climax so hard it shook me to my core.

Several orgasms later, and I was ready to pass out.

Dick had other plans.

With my face buried in the mattress and my ass high in the air, I attempted to recover from my sexual release. It had been so long since I'd felt anything like what he'd just done to me.

I felt pressure against my soaking wet mound. It damned sure wasn't a finger.

*Holy. Fucking. Hell.*

I arched my back. My mouth shot open, and I stretched my jaw so wide it hurt.

Inch by inch, he continued to fill me with dick. I groaned, and as much as I wanted to beg him to stop, I felt some pleasure in his massive girth. One inch at a time, he filled me until I had it all.

His hand pressed against my back.

I glanced over my shoulder.

"Ready?" he asked.

I felt like a man riding a bull in the rodeo, being asked by the gate attendant if he was ready to ride his way into certain death.

I nodded nonetheless.

His cock worked slowly at first, ten thick inches in, and ten out. In time, he had my pussy stretched to a new limit, and he knew it.

His hips began to pound against my ass. His balls slapped against my swollen clit. I dug my fingers into the comforter, holding on for dear life. This was what being fucked was all about, and I would have been damned to hell before I gave up or gave in.

I felt as if his cock was in my chest, but as much as it felt uncomfortable, it felt so fucking right. So god damned good. So…

Big.

I liked it so much it scared me.

I'd never had so much dick in me.

And, now that I did, I never wanted to be fucked by any less.

I had every intention of fucking Dick so good, so hard, and with such crazed passion that he'd have no choice but to make me his significant other. His favorite piece of ass, his main bitch, his…

His pace increased. My breathing became labored. I was on the verge of either dying or being sent to another place altogether, and I knew not which.

His balls pounded against my clit. His cock hit spots so deep inside of me I couldn't help but wonder how I would ever be the same. And, with a few more magical strokes, I began to burst.

*Oh. My. God.*

"Your pussy is tight as fuck," he grunted.

"I. Think. It's. Your. Big. Fucking. Dick." The words escaped my

44

lungs, one with each stroke of his massive cock.

Big dicks bring big orgasms, and they bring 'em quick. I arched my back and prepared for the mother of all orgasms. Being fucked by him felt so good. Each time his balls collided with my clit, I felt like it was coming, but it never surfaced. Stuck in sexual limbo, and fearing that I was being cheated out of what I was entitled to, I did what it seemed I always did in a pinch.

I lifted my head from the comforter. "Can you play with my ass?" I whispered.

He continued to pound away. "What?"

"My ass," I said. "Do something."

He slapped it.

And again.

I liked having my ass slapped, but it wasn't what I had in mind. I was so close, I just needed...

"Stick your finger in it?"

*There, I said it.*

I felt my ass cheeks spread apart. I chewed against my bottom lip. He did just as I asked and rubbed his finger along my wet pussy, and then slid it in my ass. It was exactly what I needed.

A tingling shot through me from my nipples to my clit.

His thick cock filled my pussy while he finger-fucked my ass. In a matter of seconds, I reached sensory overload and drifted away to my sacred sexual place.

My toes curled. His balls banged a tune on my clit. My legs shook. I pinched my nipples. His massive cock bottomed out inside of me. I gulped a breath of air. The stars aligned.

And. I. Came.

Hard.

I collapsed onto the bed.

Satisfied, exhausted, and still half-drunk, I quickly realized he was far from done fucking me.

But I was done being fucked. I was in no way prepared to be punished any more by his massive cock.

I rolled onto my back. "Cum on me."

It seemed to be a request all men enjoyed fulfilling.

I focused my drunken eyes. He looked like a dream. His six pack rippled as he stroked his glistening cock. My eyes rose to his chest. Wide, bulging, and massive, it looked like two thick slabs of tanned meat.

My mouth watered. My eyes fell to his waist.

He stroked his massive cock. "In your mouth."

I mentally agreed, but said nothing.

I spun around, fell to my knees, and looked up at his ten-inch dick. The thought of watching him stroke it to completion was a huge turn-on, and he didn't disappoint.

His clenched fist stroked from the base to the tip while I eagerly knelt at his feet. Seeing his perfectly sculpted body and his handsome face was more than enough to cause me to feel faint, but adding his jacking off to the equation made me a weakened mess.

He pressed his hand against my forehead and began to moan. With wide eyes I watched him arch his back and continue to work his full length in his hand.

I didn't want his cum on my face or in my mouth.

But I did.

Kind of.

I licked my lips in anticipation.

"You sexy little bitch," he growled.

The cum shot from the tip of his swollen dick like a rocket, every drop somehow making it into my mouth. Seeing him reach climax was insanely satisfying. Having him come in my mouth was even more so.

I wrapped my lips around the head and sucked, sending him into a frenzy. Afterward, we both relaxed on the bed, side-by-side.

"I knew you'd be a crazy little bitch," he said.

*There you go with the bitch thing again.*

I was too drunk to argue, and far too satisfied with his fat cock to start an argument. At least not this early in the game.

"You have no idea how crazy I am," I said.

It was my way of trying to convince him to keep fucking me.

And, it worked.

The next morning, he fucked me before breakfast.

And after.

When we finished the second time, I took another shower and changed into the shorts I wore to work the night before. Weakened from the sex, I knew very little, but I knew one thing for sure.

I. Was. Ruined.

# SIX

# DICK

**KNOWING** our first night together would be our only night together was difficult to accept, but it was the way things had to be. It was fun while it lasted, but forgetting her was going to be more difficult than I originally expected.

I liked her. A lot.

But. In my profession, trusting the wrong person would get me a one-way ticket to prison.

We walked through the kitchen, down the hallway, and into the garage. I needed to take her back to her car so she could go home, change, and get to work. I motioned toward the cars. A Mercedes, GT-40 Ford, BMW M5, Ferrari F12, Jeep Wrangler, and a Maserati were positioned side by side. On the far side of the cars, six motorcycles were parked. Three of the cars were mine, and the other three were in my possession, but technically weren't *mine*. I had taken them from people who owed me money.

"Which one of these do you want to take to get your car?" I asked.

She ran her fingers through her damp hair and shook it for a minute while she surveyed the inventory. "I get to pick? Out of any of them?"

It was the least I could do. "Yeah. Pick."

She lowered her hands to her hips and shifted her eyes from car to car. After a moment, she pointed to the Ferrari. "The red one."

Of all the cars, she had to pick one of the three that wasn't mine. Not only was it technically *stolen*, it was expensive as fuck. I motioned toward the car, a 700 horsepower red Ferrari F12 Berlinetta well worth the $300,000 debt it was covering.

There was one car I had no business driving, and it was the Ferrari. My pride prevented me from telling her no. I tossed my head toward it. "Get in."

I started the car and allowed it to warm up. The rumble from the V-12 engine shook the walls of the garage and provided me a reminder of its raw power. The power was only part of the reason I shouldn't be driving it. The fact it would get me tossed right back in prison was the rest.

She delicately opened the door, got inside and buckled her seatbelt. "What is it?"

"Ferrari," I said, knowing the other details were unimportant to her.

Her eyes bounced around the interior. "I like it."

Who wouldn't. I'd driven the car a few times right after I'd *repossessed* it, but hadn't so much as started it in the last six weeks. I feared the owner turned it in as stolen in an effort to get an insurance check for the theft, all in hopes of paying his debt with me. His failure to pay didn't mean he hadn't reported it stolen, it simply assured me he had no intention of paying me anytime soon.

I pulled the car out of the garage, shut the overhead door, and got back inside. "Ready?"

She grinned and nodded. "Yep."

As irritating as her attitude was at first, I found Jess to be a very satisfying person overall. She was entertaining, a great lay, and absolutely gorgeous. But. I couldn't trust anyone enough to expose them to my personal life on a regular basis. Adhering to my *single forever* mantra kept me away from prison and out of the watchful eye of the cops.

It also left me wishing from time to time that I had another profession altogether.

This was one of those times.

"I bet this thing is fast."

I checked for cross traffic and pulled out of the neighborhood. "It's stupid fast. After we get on the highway, I'll show you."

I slowly sped up to the speed limit, pulling against the Formula One style paddle shifters on the steering wheel twice. Through the open windows, the roar from the twelve-cylinder engine acted as a reminder of the car's potential.

The car was a seven speed manual shift, but as with many of the Ferrari line, it had no clutch pedal, only a + paddle to shift gears up, and a – paddle to down shift – located on each side of the steering wheel. The driver simply stepped on the gas and touched the respective paddle. It was designed to do one thing and do it well – go fast.

I stopped at the traffic light, flipped on the signal to turn right, and eased through the light. Once on the on-ramp to the highway, I glanced toward Jess. Her hair was flipping in the wind, half of it inside the car, and the other half was being sucked out through the open window. She returned my gaze, wearing an ear-to-ear grin.

She looked like a twenty-five-year-old child.

I tossed my head toward the road. "Ready?"

She looked confused. "For what?"

I stomped down on the gas pedal. The brute acceleration pinned both of us back in our seats, and remained until we reached 140 miles per hour. She screamed a joyous yelp as the exhaust note belched out the back and the road ahead rushed upon us at horrifically rapid pace. Before we merged into traffic, I released the gas pedal, applied the brakes, and began to slow the car to a moderate speed.

The car was capable of more than 200 miles per hour, but I wasn't interested in being chased by the cops or arrested for driving a stolen car. I slowed to 90 miles per hour and merged into traffic.

"Holy shit," Jess said. "This thing is fun."

"It's impossible to drive the fucker without speeding," I said.

"Do it again," she begged.

It was the least I could do for her, considering she was the first person who ever took the entire length of my cock without a moment's complaint.

I checked all three mirrors, made note of no cops, and scanned the road ahead to determine my path. "Ready?"

She grinned. "Yep."

I tapped the back of the downshift paddle four times, mashed the accelerator, and sped up from 70 to 160 almost instantly, weaving in and out of cars like a trained professional. I released the accelerator pedal and glanced at Jess. The ear-to-ear smile had either returned or never left.

"It sucks this is over," she said.

"What's that?" I asked. I no more than responded, and realized what she meant.

It did suck. My life as a professional criminal was rewarding in many respects, but disappointing in so many others. Not allowing people close to me was the most difficult part to accept, but was the one thing that kept me beyond the walls of prison.

And going back to prison wasn't an option.

She turned her head to face me. "Never seeing you again."

I nodded and opted to remain silent. I didn't like it, either, but I didn't want to talk about it.

She turned, peered out the window, and immediately screamed. "Cop!"

I checked the rearview. Sans lights, but traveling in excess of what I would guess to be 100 miles per hour, a cop was flying up behind us. I signaled and changed lanes to the right.

He changed lancs.

I signaled again and changed lanes into the exit lane.

He changed lanes.

*Fuck.*

The lights in his grille, the top of the car, and the headlights all started flashing at the same time. My asshole puckered in response.

*Son-of-a-fucking bitch.*

"Get your arm inside the window and hold on," I said.

"What?"

I pulled against the downshift paddle four times, pressed down on the gas, and flipped the window buttons to *up*. "I'm gonna outrun that prick behind us."

"The cop?" she gasped.

The car quickly sped up from 70 miles per hour to 120. "Yeah, the cop."

At 120 miles per hour, he was still close behind.

I swerved to keep from hitting a truck directly in front of us only to almost rear end a Suburban in the fast lane. Frantically, I flicked the flash-to-pass with the tips of my left fingers and swerved into the center lane with a few feet to spare. Jess screamed like she was being murdered.

"Quit fucking screaming, I can't think," I yelled.

"What the fuck are you doing?" she shouted.

I swerved to the left, barely missing a Volkswagen in the center lane. With the road ahead open, I hammered the gas and tried my best to plan well ahead, changing lanes long before I thought I needed to.

"Get the phone out of my right pocket and call Drake," I demanded.

"Okay."

Remaining remarkably calm, Jess reached into my pocket, removed my cell phone and scrolled through my contacts while I weaved in and out of four lanes at 140 miles an hour. The mid-morning Thursday traffic wasn't dense, but it sure wasn't sparse, either. The cop was a quarter of a mile behind me – still well within sight.

With my eyes fixed on the road ahead, I explained my plan. "We're coming up on Highway 1 in a minute, and we've got to hit a ninety-degree turn. We should lose him there. I'll take it at 140, he'll have to slow to about seventy."

"I found Drake," she announced.

My heart was racing, I was sweating profusely, and the thought of going back to prison was becoming more of a reality with each car we almost collided with. "Call him and tell him to open his garage door and have an empty stall for me. Tell him we're in the Ferrari and we're running from the cops," I barked.

Slumped in her seat with the phone in her lap, she shifted her eyes to me. "Only if you go out on another date."

We were flying down a highway with a marked speed limit of 65, and traveling at more than twice the speed of traffic. Objects a quarter of a mile ahead of us were reached in roughly five seconds. To describe the event as intense would be the understatement of the century.

Yet Jess seemed to care less.

"Excuse me?"

"Another date. Yes or no?"

"God damn it. Call Drake. We're coming up on Highway 1!" I demanded.

"Yes or no?"

*You crazy bitch.*

"Yes!"

She pressed her finger against the keypad and lifted the phone to her ear "Is this Drake?"

"No. He's busy. Yeah. I'm Jess. No. He's right beside me but he can't talk. No. Just listen for a sec. We're in the red Ferrari, and we're runnin' from the cops. We need to hide in your garage."

"About…"

She leaned toward the center of the car and looked at the speedometer. "Looks like about 146 right now. Dick says you need to open the garage door and make a spot for him."

"When will we be there?" she asked.

"About two minutes. Maybe less, I don't know," I responded.

"How far away is it?" she asked.

I swerved into the right lane, checked the rearview mirror, and prepared to take the exit-ramp at 140 miles per hour. "A mile from this exit. Hold on!"

"Go open the door. We'll be there in thirty seconds," she said. "And be ready to close it for us. Don't hang up."

With white knuckles and an overactive heart, I steered into the curve. The car hugged the road as we took the corner, drifting slightly, but it wasn't unmanageable. I downshifted two gears, held the throttle to the floor, and merged onto the next highway. A quick check of the mirror showed the police car taking the corner much faster than he probably should have.

"Cop just wrecked!" Jess shouted.

*Thank God.*

"We're taking the next exit," I exclaimed. "Hold on again."

"Two cops behind us," Jess said. She wagged her finger toward the windshield. "And there's one on the right at the side of the road."

*Fuck.*

"We're going to act like we're going past this exit, and then I'm gonna take it at the last second. Grab my pistol. It's under my shirt."

She didn't hesitate. As if it were an everyday occurrence, she lifted my shirt, pulled the pistol from the waist of my pants, and held it in her hand.

Our exit was fast approaching.

*Fifteen seconds.*

Two cars were behind us, and I was stretching the distance slightly. The cop car ahead was speeding into traffic in anticipation of us catching up with him.

"Hold onto it. If we wreck, hand me that fucker, get out, and throw your hands up in the air. You can claim I kidnapped you, I don't give a fuck. But just so you know, they're not arresting me."

I expected her to gasp. Scream. Tell me no. Go ballistic and start babbling incoherently. She did none of those things.

"Okay," she said calmly. "But I'm not telling 'em that. We're in this together. I'm the one that told you to go fast."

*Interesting…*

"We're taking this exit, and it's gonna be a bitch," I assured her. "Grab ahold of something."

I gripped the wheel tight, bracing myself for what I was sure to be a crash.

With two cops behind us half a mile, and one slightly ahead and on the right, I got as close to the exit as I could, holding the middle lane as if we were heading for the open road. At the last instant, I touched the brakes, fell behind him, and swerved through three lanes toward the exit on the far right.

The car slowed considerably from the force of the ninety-degree turn.

I downshifted three times, pushed the throttle to the floor, and screamed as we took the exit at a speed well in excess of what was safe.

"Fuuuuuucccckkkkkkk!" I cried out as the rear of the car hopped up and down, skipping across the pavement like the rocks I used to skip across the pond as a kid.

The car fishtailed a little, and I slowed slightly. I somehow recovered, and hit the gas again. By the grace of God, we made it through the curve without wrecking. The cop, on the other hand, shot well past the exit.

Jess fumbled for the phone. After finding it, she held it to her ear. "Still there? Yeah. No. One of them wrecked. Yeah. We just got off on 35th. Okay. Okay. I'll tell him."

"Drake's at the door waiting."

I had plenty to worry about. My focus was – and had to remain – the road, driving, and what obstacles were well ahead of us. I couldn't help but admire Jess' calm demeanor and acceptance of everything that was going on.

I slowed to roughly 60 miles per hour, took a narrow left, and downshifted four times. After pegging the throttle and tapping the paddle shifter a few times, we screeched into Drake's neighborhood. A few seconds later, and we were in his driveway. I checked over my shoulder. Jess did the same.

I pulled the car into the garage, let out a long sigh, and turned to face Jess. As Drake powered the garage door down, Jess grinned her ear-to-ear smile.

"What?" I asked.

"That was crazy."

I rolled my eyes. "Sure as fuck was."

The driver's door flew open.

Drake stood outside the door with a half-eaten hot dog in his hand.

He was in his mid-thirties, but acted and appeared to be just shy of fifty. He was of average height and average weight, but his hair made him seem much older. The shoulder-length strands of filth were brown with streaks of grey, and his long goatee was solid white. He wore the same thing every time I saw him, regardless of whether he was at home, a club, or eating at one of the Vietnamese soup kitchens he liked to frequent.

A robe and matching pajama pants. Plaid was the choice of the day.

Everything he did had a price attached to it. It didn't matter how simple or how difficult the task, he simply did nothing for free. He was one of the last people I wanted to see, but his house was the only place I felt I could safely reach without wrecking the car or being arrested.

"How's it hangin', Dick?"

I stepped out of the car and nodded. "Low, as always. Appreciate this."

He brushed his long greying hair behind his ears and peered over the top of the car. "God damn, Dick. Where'd you get this one?"

I waved my finger back and forth between them. "Jess, this is Drake. Drake, Jess."

Dressed in her work clothes from the previous night, Jess walked around the front of the car, pushed the pistol into the waist of her shorts, and examined his attire. Her eyes fell to the hot dog. Drake poked the wiener in his mouth and held it between his teeth.

"Nice to meet you." He extended his hand.

She seemed to weigh the risk. After a long pause, she shook his hand.

He eye-fucked her for a moment, took a bite of the hot dog, then turned to face me. "I'll keep the Ferrari well-hidden for ya, and you can take the 'Vette I just bought, but I need you to do something for me."

*What a surprise.*

My heart was still racing a hundred miles an hour, and I wasn't in the mood for Drake's demands – but I wasn't in a position to negotiate. "What's that?"

He clutched the lapels of his robe, pulled it closed, and grinned. He shook the hotdog at me as he spoke. "Drop something off. But she's staying here 'till you get back."

"Excuse me?" Jess snapped.

He turned toward Jess for an instant. "You're staying here 'till he gets back."

Jess' eyes shot to me. I shrugged and cleared my throat. "Where?"

"Chinatown."

*Fuck.*

"Who?"

"What's it matter?" he asked. "You owe me."

"Who?"

"Duc."

"Duc? Like *The Duc*?"

He nodded.

*Fuck.*

I tried to act like it didn't matter. It mattered. A lot. I wondered how convincing I looked. "One delivery? That's it?"

He poked the remaining hot dog in his mouth, chewed it, and responded before swallowing. "One drop off, and a pick up. An exchange, of sorts."

He ran his fingers through his greasy hair while he finished chewing the wiener. His eyes told me what his mouth had yet to say. There was a reason he hadn't done this deal yet; I was sure of it.

I kept my business out of Chinatown for a reason. "In and out deal, huh?"

He returned a smug grin. "In and out."

"He ready now?"

"As ready as he's gonna get."

I looked at Jess and did my best to apologize without apologizing. "We'll go out this weekend."

She returned a shitty glare.

I shifted my eyes to Drake. "Grab the keys. And when did you get a 'Vette?"

"Same time I got this package. Two days ago," he said. "Be right back."

He sauntered to the door and went inside the house, leaving Jess and me alone in the garage. The fact he had the package for two days and had yet to deliver it made the little job much less appealing.

"I've got to stay here with the hotdog guy? And what was that entire running from the cops shit about? Entrepreneur, my ass," she hissed.

I raised my hands in an effort to calm her. "I've just got to drop something off for him and bring something back. It's just how Drake is. When I get back, we'll take the 'Vette and be gone. Just hang here with him for an hour. I'll be in and out. You can play slot machines. It'll be fun."

"Slot machines?"

I pulled out my wallet and grabbed five $100 bills and handed them to her. "Yeah. He's got a little casino in there. You'll have fun."

She counted the money. "You'll be back in an hour?"

"One hour. Maybe less."

"And then you'll take me to my car?"

"As soon as I get back."

She let out a sigh. "You owe me. Big time."

After the way she handled the little run-in with the law, I didn't disagree.

# SEVEN

# JESS

**"HOW** long have you known ol' Dick?" Drake asked.

I pushed my hand into the pocket of my shorts and pinched the $500 Dick gave me between my fingers. "I just met him."

I was more attracted to Dick after the police chase. A bad boy who talked a long line of shit – but couldn't back it up – was annoying. Dick, on the other hand, was the real deal. Police chases, guns, Ferraris, using rich friend's houses for hideouts, and now a mysterious delivery to Chinatown?

Dick may have been a dick and unwilling to commit, but he was exactly what I desired in a man.

I was going to have a difficult time forgetting the Dicks.

Drake opened the refrigerator and pulled out a package of what appeared to be bologna. "Just met him a few minutes ago, or just met him recently?"

"On Monday."

He held the package of lunchmeat at arm's length. "Bologna?"

"No, thank you."

"Monday, huh?"

"Yep."

"What do you think?" He rolled up a piece of bologna and poked

63

half of it into his mouth.

"About what?"

He chewed the bologna, swallowed it, and gazed at the other half as if it wasn't at all what he expected it to be. He unrolled it, stared at it for a moment, and turned toward me.

I had no idea what he wanted. He alternated glances between me and the remaining lunchmeat several times. Eventually, I shrugged. It was all I could think to do.

He walked to the other side of the kitchen, sniffed the bologna, and shook his head. He turned to face me. "Dick."

It took me a minute to realize he was responding to the question I had asked earlier.

"Oh. He's fun."

He tossed the uneaten half of the bologna in the trash. He stared down at the package he was holding for some time, and after a lengthy mental struggle, tossed it in the trash. A trip back to the refrigerator produced a package of cheese, and the same process continued.

He rolled a piece of cheese into a tube, ate half of it, and nodded his head as if it provided the satisfaction he was hoping to get from the bologna.

He offered me the cheese. "Cheese?"

"No, thank you."

He ate the other half of the cheese slice and closed the refrigerator door. "Follow me."

I did as he said and followed him through a very contemporary living room that was decorated with green leather furniture, chrome and glass end tables, and a large matching coffee table. Abstract art hung from the walls and random sculptures were placed about.

It seemed like something I would expect to see in the home of a big Hollywood producer, but not in Austin, Texas. Not even in the ritzy Mount Bonnell neighborhood we were in.

We walked down a long hallway, past a few rooms, and into what was obviously his casino. Two blackjack tables, a craps table, and a few dozen slot machines filled the large room.

He sat down at a slot machine. "Fun, huh? Suppose that's a matter of perception."

The way he responded or commented on a subject several minutes after we discussed it was confusing. I decided to keep to myself, and hoped Dick wasn't gone for very long.

He reached into the pocket of his robe, removed the package of cheese, and placed it beside the slot machine. He then pulled out a large bundle of $100 bills, and poked several in the machine. "Gamble?"

I had gambled before, but it wasn't something I could afford to do. As much as I needed to keep the $500 Dick gave me for food, clothes, and other necessities, I wanted to try my luck at gambling even more.

I glanced around the room. "Can I?"

"Long as you've got money."

"What happens if I win?"

He glared at me.

Assuming he'd pay me if I won – and that I insulted him by asking – I pulled one of the $100 bills from my pocket, fed it into the machine, and began playing.

To describe the morning as surreal seemed so cliché, but I didn't know what else to call it. Being chased by the cops in a Ferrari, ending up in Mount Bonnell amidst $5,000,000 homes, and watching a greasy-haired guy in a robe eat rotten bologna only to end up in his personal casino watching him eat slice after slice of cheese was nothing short of bizarre.

I pushed the button on the machine and watched as all the little characters were falling into place on the screen. Drake peeled another slice of the cheese from the block, pulled his phone from his pocket, and nibbled on the cheese as he answered.

I pinched myself.

"Dick. You on your way? Whoa. Hold on. Slow down." He stood up, grabbed another slice of cheese, and began to pace the floor. "No, make sure it gets to Duc. I don't give a damn. No. Duc. And when you get to the car, count the money. There should be a million. No more and damned sure no less. Oh, and make sure your fingerprints aren't on that case. Well, I didn't think about it. Alright."

He put the phone in his pajama pants pocket, pulled his robe closed, and sat down. I may have been a dumb waitress, but it was pretty easy to see that this guy was a rich fucking weirdo, and Dick was no entrepreneur. Nervously, I continued to play the machine.

I had no idea what the premise of the machine was, but there were five rows of characters and each row was three characters high. I played for almost an hour, and watched as my balance went down to $60, back up to $120, and steadily continued to drop.

After telling myself I'd stop when it got to $50, I pushed the button and hoped for a win. Three matching tombstones came up. Each one spun in circles, and the machine congratulated me for making it to the *bonus round.*

*Fuck yes.*

Excited and hoping to win my $100 back, I glanced at Drake. He had moved over to another machine, and half the cheese was gone. I

66

pushed the button and won $124. I pushed it again and won $27.

By the time I was done with my 13 spins, my balance was $623.57.

I pressed the *cash out* button and waited for the receipt.

"So what do I do if I'm ready to quit playing?"

"Give me the ticket."

I waked over to him and handed him the ticket. He glanced at it, reached into his pocket, and counted out $630.

"I don't have any ones, just $100's," I explained.

He shrugged and pressed the button on his machine. "Don't worry about it.

I shoved the money in my pocket.

I had pre-breakfast and post-breakfast sex, rode in a Ferrari, was chased by the cops, I got to hold a real gun, and I'd just won $630 at crazy lunchmeat man's house.

Best. Day. Ever.

A familiar voice caused me to turn around.

"There's something in the kitchen for you," Dick said.

*Thank God you're back.*

"My man Dick," Drake stood up and grabbed the cheese. "Everything go slick?"

"Suppose so," Dick said with a nod. He tossed his head toward the door. "C'mon, Jess. We're leaving."

"Not gonna stick around and talk?" Drake asked as he approached Dick.

"No. I've got to get her to work."

The remaining cheese went up for offer. "Cheese?"

"No. I don't want your fucking cheese. Or a hotdog. Or bologna. I want to get the fuck out of here, get her to work, and try and forget cops and gooks."

I stepped to Dick's side.

"Did Duc rove you rong time?" Drake asked jokingly.

"Fuck you, Drake. It's in the kitchen. All of it. I'll bring the car back as soon as I can."

"What about the Ferrari?"

Dick shrugged. "Let me think on that for a bit."

Drake patted my shoulder with his cheese hand. "Jess, I must say, the pleasure was mine."

"It was nice to meet you," I said, although he was really gross.

"You want your $500 back?" I asked as we walked toward the garage.

"Did you gamble?"

"Uh huh."

"If you gambled and you didn't lose it, you can keep it."

It probably didn't seem like much to him, but $1030 was life changing for me.

I shook hands with Drake, but Dick didn't. After we got in the car I admired him without staring – stealing glances as he drove. He seemed annoyed, and I wondered how the Chinatown delivery went. Obviously not very well, I decided.

Halfway to my car, I broke the silence. "Something wrong?"

He seemed to find the question entertaining, coughing out a laugh before he responded. "Typical day in the life of Dick."

"Tomorrow's Friday. When are we going out?"

He tapped his fingers against the steering wheel. "How's your work schedule?"

I thought of the $1030 in my pocket and realized I could actually afford to take off early. "I'm scheduled to work, but I can get off early either night."

"Let's do it tomorrow."

*Let's do it tomorrow.* It sounded like a burden. As attracted as I was to him, I didn't want the date to be an annoyance or something he didn't think he would enjoy.

"You don't have to take me out. We can call it even. I shouldn't have made you agree to it."

He changed lanes, adjusted the rearview mirror, and stared into it for a minute. "It's been a fucked up day, Jess. Sorry if I'm not jumping up and fucking down about our date."

My mouth went dry just a little. The whole thing seemed forced. I wanted him to like me, but my self-pride wouldn't allow him to treat me like I was an aggravation.

I stared out the side window. "Just forget it."

"Forget what?"

"The date."

"What are you talking about?" he snapped back.

"Forget it. I don't want to go out with you again if you don't want to go."

I sounded like such a girl. I didn't care. I continued to stare out the window, listening to his breathing, which was labored and sounded angry.

"I want to go out."

I turned to face him. I heard him just fine, but I wanted to hear him say it again. "Excuse me?"

"I want to go out with you."

I wanted more. "Why?"

"You've got a nice little pussy."

*Are you fucking kidding me?*

I glared "Are you fucking…"

"And you're fun," he interrupted.

It wasn't much, but it was a start. "You think I'm fun?"

He shot me his shitty little smirk and nodded.

I smiled. "I think you're fun, too."

*And when Friday gets here, I'm going to rock your world, Dick.*

# EIGHT

# DICK

**THERE** was no way I was going to let him fuck me on the diamond, regardless of how I got my hands on it. "I don't give a fuck what your little wholesale chart says. It's not a wholesale piece. Look at it. My sources tell me it's 10.22 carats, D color, and IF clarity. It's a *gem*, no pun intended."

"And there's no laser inscription," I added. "An easy piece to move."

"Let me make a call to an investor," he said.

I shrugged. "Make all the calls you want."

He walked to the back of the store and returned in a few minutes. His face was covered in a guilty smirk. Apparently, his call went well. "I need to take the stone to the back. I should just be a moment."

"You're not taking that rock anywhere."

He was five-foot tall, bald, and walked like a duck. With his jeweler's glasses over his eyes and his eyeglasses propped on top of his head, he returned a rather confused look.

"I'd like to inspect it with a scope. The refraction of--"

"Bring your scope up here. Or take me back there. Either one."

He pressed the switch on the wall, activating the electronic door lock and securing the front door. With the stone cradled in his hand like he was carrying a pressure sensitive bomb, he turned toward the rear of the store. "Follow me."

After a rather lengthy inspection under a microscope, he removed the diamond, placed it to the side, and sighed.

"I'd go $2,500,000."

I shook my head. "I'd take $3,000,000."

"It's…I…" he stammered.

"It's what? I tell you what it is. It's fucking huge. It's flawless. And it's one of a kind. Wholesale is $2,245,100 at 10 carats. At 10.22, it's $2,295,000. But, like I said…"

He picked up the diamond, admired it, and placed it on the folded cloth. "$2,750,000."

"Three."

"But…"

"But nothing," I said. "I'll toss that motherfucker in the Colorado river before I sell it for anything less."

He quickly reached for the stone and covered it with his hand. "You certainly will not. I'll go three. It'll take me several days to get the funds. Investors, you know."

I fought against the urge to smile at the $2,000,000 profit I would make from the transaction. "Understood." I tilted my head toward the diamond. "Give me the rock and call me when you're ready."

He set the jeweler's glasses aside. "I'd rather keep it here. In the safe."

"I bet you would." I pointed to the stone. "Call me when you're ready."

He reluctantly handed me the stone, his eyes glued to it the entire time. He grimaced as I wrapped it in the cloth and shoved it into my pocket.

"Three days at the most. Maybe two," he said as he reached for the door switch.

I caught a reflection in the mirror behind him that looked like a white Nissan GT-R Nismo driving by. My asshole puckered. I spun around and scanned the parking lot.

*Nothing.*

Although I was rarely nervous about anything, I told myself that was the case. I must have been nervous. After all, I had three million reasons to be nervous.

"I'll be waiting for your call."

"Very well," he said with a smile.

I turned toward the front door just as the magnetic lock clicked, unlocking it for free passage. I pushed the door open, walked to my car, and reached for the door handle.

A sharp pain shot down my spine, followed by a blinding light, then everything went black.

# NINE

# JESS

**OUR** date was in no way what I expected – or hoped for – but it led me to believe Dick may be seeing me as slightly more than a simple piece of ass.

He pulled the earmuff away from my right ear. "Squeeze the trigger. Don't yank it."

I nodded. My father was in the military, and growing up on a farm as the only sister to three brothers, a gun wasn't anything new to me. I'd fired them many times, but never in an indoor range. I steadied the gun, aligned the sights, and squeezed the trigger.

The recoil from the 9mm wasn't near as brutal as the .45 caliber my father taught me to shoot with. I stared at the target, slightly disappointed with my performance – the rip in the paper target wasn't exactly where I'd pointed, but it was close. I fired another. And another. In a matter of seconds, the slide stayed open, a reminder that the 17-round magazine was empty.

I glanced at Dick.

"Not bad," he said with a nod. "Definitely not your first time."

"Not at all," I said. "My father was a Marine. And, I grew up on a farm."

He reeled the target in and inspected it. "Impressive."

I studied the three-inch long gash on the side of his forehead. "So, are you going to tell me what happened?"

"Just like I told you earlier. Misunderstanding."

I knew better than to pry. There was no doubt that Dick was involved in some shady stuff, and as with most people who chose the life of an outlaw, he kept his criminal life private.

"Okay."

He pulled off my target, placed a new one on the clip, and ran the it out to twenty-five feet.

"Put on your ears," he said.

I pulled the earmuffs over my ears and put on my glasses. Seventeen shots were fired as fast as he was able to pull the trigger. He placed the pistol down, reeled the target in, and inspected it.

All of the rounds were within a few inches of each other. I knew enough about firing a pistol to know he was as good as my father, and he was as good as the US Marine Corps had ever seen.

I pointed at the shredded paper. "Wow."

He shrugged. "Lots of practice."

"I guess so."

We alternated back and forth, each taking turns shooting at various targets. I appreciated that he wanted to use the same lane, and enjoy the time we spent at the range – instead of getting two lanes and making it a less personal experience.

After we fired all of the ammunition, he glanced around the empty range. "So, you about ready to eat?"

"Sure," I said.

He was dressed in a V-neck tee shirt, jeans, and dress shoes, which was much different than the other two times I'd seen him. His muscular

SCOTT HILDRETH

physique was undeniable in the clothes he was wearing, and staring was something I had to consciously try to keep myself from doing.

The tee shirt clung to his wide chest as he placed the pistols, glasses, and earmuffs in the padded case. After cleaning up all of the trash, he picked up the gun case and patted me on the shoulder.

"Ready?"

"You sure everything's okay?" I asked.

"What do you mean?"

"You sure whatever hit your head didn't do some damage?"

"I'm fine, why?"

I knew he hadn't changed – because people never do – but I wondered if the way he looked at me had. Or at least I hoped.

"Nothing," I said, not wanting to scare him away.

I walked slightly behind him, acting preoccupied with everything, although I wasn't. I liked watching him walk, and imagined what other people thought when they saw him for the first time.

Seeing him was intimidating, but hearing him talk was just about as bad. He was the type of man who commanded everyone's attention whether he realized it or not.

He unlocked the car and put the case in the trunk. "What are you in the mood for?"

I wanted him to fuck me. I was well aware that sex with me meant nothing to him, and that whatever we were doing wasn't permanent – but as far as I was concerned it was all the more reason to be fucking and not eating a cheeseburger or talking over a glass of wine.

"Dick."

He shot me a confused look. "What?"

"No," I said. "You asked what I was in the mood for. I want some

77

dick, Dick."

"I can arrange that," he responded flatly.

I lowered myself into the seat and buckled my seatbelt, feeling like something was wrong. I doubted a person like Dick ended up with a three-inch hole in his forehead without there being a story to go along with it.

I knew better than to ask again, but I couldn't help but wonder. "Let's eat something light and go back to your place and bone."

My idea bounced around inside the quiet car for some time before he responded.

"Sounds good," he said.

No smart remark. No *I'm in charge, you'll do what I say* response. Just a *sounds good*. I wanted him to get in another high-speed chase with the cops, pull over and fuck me on the hood of the car, or say he had to rob a bank really quick just so I'd feel like he was doing alright. I wondered if any of those possibilities could come to fruition.

What originally appealed to me about Dick – besides his very obvious dick – was that he seemed like the ultimate bad boy. Not a punk kid with an attitude, or a man with a desire to simply act like an asshole, but a true bad boy through and through.

Now, he seemed like an average guy. Well, one who was covered in muscles and was rocking a massive cock.

The only thing I knew that might bring him out of his slump was a blowjob. A good dick sucking seemed to be a cure-all for whatever was wrong with a man – at least the men I knew. I took my chances and unbuckled my seatbelt.

The warning buzzer began to ding.

"What the fuck are you doing?" he snarled.

I felt it would be best that I didn't respond. Maybe, I thought, it would bring out the asshole in him. Make him revert back to normal. I reached to unbuckle his belt, and he squirmed in his seat and gave me a shitty glare.

"Answer me."

I had yet to wrap my lips around it, and he was already acting like he was feeling better.

I returned a shitty glare of my own, and pulled his half-stiff cock from his jeans.

"Just drive," I said.

"You might not want to do that," he warned.

"Why?"

"My cock is angry right now."

"Feed me every angry inch of it," I said.

He let out a sigh. "You asked."

With one hand on the steering wheel and one on the back of my head, he forced the tip of his stiff cock past my lips.

I had always considered myself versed in the art of sucking dick, and I'd never encountered one I couldn't swallow. Convinced Dick's wasn't going to be the first, I tried to start off slow and prepare my throat for what was sure to come.

Apparently, he didn't get the memo.

Immediately, the tip of his dick began banging against the back of my throat. With watering eyes and a convulsing gag reflex I never knew I had, I sucked his cock the best that I was able.

He was right.

He was angry.

Most women would find what he was doing to me to be either

repulsive or a disgraceful. Some might even describe it as abusive.

Me?

I loved it when a man shoved his cock down my throat. The bigger the better. It brought out the best in me.

I pulled my mouth off his dick and looked up at him. "Fuck yes. Fuck my mouth."

"Shut the fuck up," he snarled.

He grabbed the back of my head and shoved my face in his lap.

With his dick covered in my saliva, and my throat finally prepped for the occasion, I flattened my tongue against the bottom of the shaft, and eagerly swallowed every inch of him.

His hips worked in unison with me, forcing himself up when my mouth was traveling down. In a matter of minutes, my pussy started to ache. Throbbing and tingling, it was screaming for some cock of its own. I wanted to beg, but I didn't.

Instead, I sucked harder. Faster. More aggressively. In response, he pulled against my hair, lifting my head from his lap.

"I'm going to fuck the shit out of you," he growled.

He pulled the car over and all but yanked me from inside. Nervously, I looked around, wondering what well-lit parking lot he'd landed in. I glanced at the building. A red and white circle plastered to the side made me grin.

*Target.*

At 7:00 on a Friday night. Granted, we were parked in the rear of the lot, and behind the building, but we were there in broad daylight.

*Perfect.*

With both of us standing outside of his car, and his cock standing at attention, he lifted my dress to my waist, pulled against my panties, and eventually ripped them in two.

I'd never been one for public sex, and in fact, wondered if the opportunity ever presented itself if I would be able to perform. When he pushed my head into the seat of his car and shoved me full of dick, I got my answer.

I loved it.

His hips pounded against my ass while he forced inch after inch of his thick cock into me. With each stroke I let out a grunt of satisfaction, imagining random soccer moms and single fathers happening by only to see me getting fucked senseless in the parking lot.

*This is so hot.*

The size of his dick made being fucked an entirely different experience. I was no newcomer to sex, being fucked hard, or being bent over and hate fucked – which was exactly what he was doing.

Having Dick fuck me redefined everything I thought I knew about sex.

While filled with his cock, I never wanted it to end. It was painful, erotic, magical, beyond compare, and one hundred fucking percent satisfying.

I felt him withdraw from my pussy. I wondered what I did wrong? Why he would end such a wonderful thing? Even if we were in the parking lot of a Target Superstore, stopping in the middle of something that felt so good should be criminal.

Further proof that my suspicions were correct.

His hand between my legs made me jump. He rubbed his palm against my soaking wet pussy and wiped my juices along the crack of my ass. I felt slight pressure against my anus. And then a little more.

"Whoa. Whoa." I begged. "No. There's…"

Slowly, he began to slide his cock inside.

*Oh. My. God.*

My entire body began to tingle.

"Fuck it." I took a deep breath.

"Do it," I growled. "Just. Take. It. Easy."

Slowly, he began to fuck me in the ass. Apparently, whoever hit him in the head got away without being punished, and I was paying the price for it. I hated the fact that he got hit, but I was glad to act as the means of relief for his suppressed frustration.

I bit against my bottom lip.

As his thick shaft worked in and out of my ass with care, I felt myself begin to reach climax. I buried my face in the seat of his car, reached back with my right hand, and began to rub my clit feverishly.

I closed my eyes and prayed for him to never stop fucking me. A few seconds later, I burst into an orgasm to end all orgasms, wailing my satisfaction into the small space inside of his car. An instant later, I felt him release his warmth into my ass.

I collapsed face-first into the seat.

He chuckled. "I just butt fucked you in the parking lot of a fucking grocery store."

I caught my breath and turned around. He was buckling his belt. The tingling sensation in my ass acted as a constant reminder of what had just happened.

"Yeah. You did," I said. "And I loved it."

"I decided something right before I came," he said.

"What's that?"

"Well, this chick was driving by, and she was rubbernecking. You know, she slowed way down and was watching me fuck you. And I didn't know what to fucking do. So, I waved at her. And, I mean, I'm nuts deep in your ass. It's fucking 7:00. It's daylight, and I'm butt fucking you with your head all shoved into the seat of the car and your ass in the air."

"So what'd you decide?"

"Oh. I decided that you're alright."

*Alright.* I found it heartwarming that an asshole like him would say such a thing. "Just alright?"

"Yeah." He brushed the wrinkles from his shirt and shoved his hands into his front pockets. "So, you busy tomorrow?"

"Night?"

He shrugged. "Whatever."

I was scheduled to work, but I didn't care. Not. One. Bit. "No," I said. "Not at all."

"Cool."

I got out of the car, waddled to the passenger side door, and carefully lowered my sore ass into the seat. He got in and closed the door.

"Ready?"

"Every time you ask me that, something crazy happens," I said.

"Welcome to my life," he said.

I didn't know if he meant it to be a formal invitation, but I took it as one.

And, I was *ready.*

# TEN

# DICK

**STEALING** drug money is one of the easiest ways to get killed, but the cash return for the typical job is tenfold what any bank job would produce.

Contrary to what is shown on television shows and movies, most banks don't keep much more than $100,000 on hand. Smaller neighborhood banks may not have $10,000. Robbing a bank of their cash on hand is a huge risk with minimal return.

Safe deposit boxes often provide a much better return versus risk, but unless someone has provided information regarding a particular box's contents, knowing what's inside prior to the theft is impossible.

I needed the money I lost in the diamond deal, and a little more.

A million more.

According to my sources, the one-bedroom shack in the barrio was going to have two million dollars in cash in it with one person guarding the money between 9:00 and 10:00 pm.

If they were wrong, and there was more than one person, I'd be dead in a matter of seconds. A certain portion of the successes a thief has must be attributed to blind luck, and I was hoping mine hadn't run out.

The small house was amongst many others like it in a prominently poor neighborhood in the barrio. It wasn't uncommon for homes such as the one I was going to raid to be used for a one-time drug deal, and more often than not they weren't even owned. They were abandoned homes that were used by the dealers for the amount of time it took to obtain the drugs, distribute them, and haul out the proceeds.

Often without running water or electricity, they used candles and battery powered lights for illumination.

Based on the dim flicker around the edge of the window covering, my guess was this particular home was using candles.

I just hoped there wasn't more than one person present.

Dressed in black SWAT gear and carrying a Heckler and Koch MP5 9mm submachine gun, I looked like a police officer. The backpack I carried didn't make me look very official, but it would aid me in a quick escape. The fake business cards in my wallet identified me as a Federal Drug Enforcement Agent. The badge on my vest was as close to official as could ever be produced.

But if the home was full of occupants, credentials wouldn't matter.

Gunshots would be fired long before I would ever have an opportunity to produce them.

I lowered my shoulders and hustled through the yard. Once at the back door, I listened for voices and heard nothing. One deep breath, half exhaled, and…

Holding the machinegun at the ready, I kicked the door in.

A Hispanic man standing in the dimly lit kitchen pulled a revolver from his holster but didn't point it at me. He appeared to be no more than 17 years old. There was no doubt in my mind the bulletproof vest I wore would stop the caliber of slug the revolver would fire, but I wasn't in the risk taking business.

"No se mueven, yo soy un agente federal!" I shouted.

*Don't move, I'm a federal agent!*

His eyes shot wide.

He raised the pistol.

I fired one round into his shoulder, knocking him to the floor.

"Es nadie en la casa?" I asked as I reached for his pistol.

*Is anyone else here?*

He shook his head and groaned.

I pointed the silenced submachinegun at his head. "Tu dinero o tu vida," I warned.

*Your money or your life.*

His eyes motioned to the adjoining room.

After determining he didn't have another weapon, and taking his cell phone, I left him bleeding on the kitchen floor and walked into the next room. In the corner of the room on the carpet was a pile of money.

*Fuck.*

It appeared to be all small bills.

$2,000,000 in $100 bills would easily fit in the backpack and would weigh only 40 pounds. The pile in front of me was either much more than $2,000,000, or it was very small bills.

I pulled the canvas bag from the backpack, filled it with as much money as I could carry, and filled the backpack.

I slung the machinegun over my shoulder, slipped my arms through the straps of the backpack, and shouldered the canvas bag.

When I walked back through the kitchen, the man was sitting with his back against the wall, clearly in shock. I pulled the man's phone from my pocket and dialed 911. As the operator answered, I stepped through the door and tossed the phone in the yard.

If I made it to my car, I'd be home free.

And, after a few hours of counting, I'd know if I had enough money to meet the commitments I'd made to myself.

*** 

Zane shook his head. "Why do you do this each time we do business? There's a reason everyone calls you Dick, isn't there?"

"It's my fucking name, asshole."

"Spot is $489,800. Each. So, that's $1,959,200 for four. What the fuck do you do with all of this shit anyway?"

"That's none of your fucking business. Make it $1,900,000. I like even numbers."

"It's worth more. Like I said--"

"Save it," I interrupted. "You got this shit at about $300 an ounce. You're making a million and a half profit, and there's no taxes, no questions asked, and no fucking IRS involvement. Legal money laundering. Take the $1,900,000 before I go somewhere else."

He rubbed his jaw between his thumb and forefinger. "You've got the cash?"

I cocked an eyebrow. "Come on, Zane. Have I ever fucked you over?"

"Can't say you have. You always try and fuck me on price, but you're a man of your word, no doubt."

I shrugged and turned up my palms. "So, we got a deal?"

"I get tired of dealing with you, but your money's good. Sure. Four for $1,900,000. When do you want to pick them up?"

I glared at him. "What the fuck, Dude? I'm here now."

"You've got the cash with you?"

I nodded. "What do you think I carried in here? Dirty fucking clothes?"

After weighing the money, I left with four 400-ounce gold bars. It seemed ludicrous paying almost $2,000,000 for 100 pounds of gold, but it was the equivalent of cash, and it couldn't be traced.

Typically, some – if not all – of the money I ended up with could be traced back to a point of origin, and the end users certainly didn't need or deserve to be questioned about how they obtained it.

I did what I did for a reason, and although some would say there was no justification to steal, manipulate, or swindle, I disagreed. I wouldn't hesitate to resort to whatever means were required to protect my investments or to shield the causes I supported from legal ramifications.

***

I pulled into the driveway, parked, and confirmed the address matched what was on my phone. I got out, opened the trunk, and retrieved a gym bag with two of the gold bars in it. I slipped my arm through the strap and walked up the sidewalk to the front porch.

A matter of seconds after the doorbell rang, a woman answered the door.

She looked exhausted, but there was no doubt she was the woman from the many articles I had read.

"You're Missy Wilson, right?"

Her look of exhaustion quickly turned to fear. "I uhhm. I'm sorry, do I know you?"

I shook my head and adjusted the bag on my shoulder. "No ma'am. I read about you in the newspaper, and I saw your GoFundMe on

Facebook. Your son suffered from Meconium Aspiration Syndrome."

"Suffers. Yes. What can I help you with?"

I lowered the bag from my shoulder. "Accept this. If you'd do that, it'd make me a happy man."

Her eyes fell to the bag, and then rose to meet my sorrowful gaze. "What is it?"

"It's gold. It's roughly a million dollars' worth, so you'll need to keep it in a safe place."

Her eyes went wide. She stared back at me. It appeared she didn't know whether to say *thank you* or *fuck you*.

"Honey, who is it?" I heard a man's voice ask from inside the house.

Her rather large husband stepped into the opening of the door. "Something I can do for you?"

I'd seen his face in the newspaper article. "You're Mark."

"Yeah."

I unzipped the bag. "There's fifty pounds of gold here. About a million dollars' worth. I saw you were taking donations, and had only raised $25,000. Your medical bills were over $500,000. I'd like to donate this."

He glanced down at the gold, stared for a moment, and then met my gaze.

I nodded my head toward the bag. "It's not as heavy as you'd think."

He glanced to his left, and then to his right. He fixed his eyes on mine. "You're serious."

"Yes, Sir. Keep whatever's left over for, I don't know." I shrugged. "Maybe use it for his education."

He glanced at his wife. Tears were rolling down her cheeks.

"I really don't want to go until you take that inside," I said. "And just so you know, you can melt it, cut it into pieces, whatever. It's worth the same no matter what. Each bar is about half a million bucks."

He exhaled. His lips parted. He tried twice, but couldn't seem to speak. I didn't need him to. I shifted my eyes toward his wife. She was still crying.

I nodded toward the bag.

She tried to lift it, couldn't, and tugged against the handle until she dragged it inside the door.

And I turned and walked away.

# ELEVEN

# JESS

**"IT'S** really complicated," Dick said. "And it's best that you just don't know. Can we leave it at that?"

"I thought we already did. I didn't ask, you offered."

We sat in a restaurant, talking. It seemed he was wanting to reach an agreement with me that I wouldn't ask about his profession, but I hadn't since we were at Drake's house, and I had no intention of doing so again.

I felt my asking seemed to annoy him, and that was exactly what I didn't want to do.

He twisted the tips of his chopsticks through the soup and raised a bundle of noodles to his mouth. "I just think you're pretty cool. For a chick, anyway."

*For a chick?*

It seemed so sexist. "What? Like girls can't be cool? What the fuck, Dick?"

"I said you were cool."

"For a chick."

"Yeah."

"Whatever, Dick. Thanks. *I guess.*"

He grinned, raised the noodles in acknowledgement, and then poked them into his mouth. As he ate, I dug through my bowl with my spoon. Eating the soup with sticks was impossible, and fitting two-foot long noodles in the one-inch wide spoon seemed more impossible yet.

I decided to sip the broth until it was gone, and then deal with the noodles.

"Do you want a fork?" he asked.

"Is it legal? Can you use a fork in one of these places?"

He chuckled. "I thought you were a criminal?"

I shook my head. "I'm not a criminal in a criminal sense, at least not yet. I just don't like cops."

He lowered his chopsticks. "Oh, is that it? Why?"

I placed my spoon to the side of my bowl. "They're supposed to serve and protect, right?"

"That's what it says on the sides of their cars, anyway."

"Well, tell that to every kid they end up shooting for no reason. I can't log onto the internet without MSN's newsfeed giving me another link to look at. Always the same shit. Some cop shot another unarmed citizen. And they always find in favor of the cop. They're never held accountable. Except in some closed-door hearing. It's like they're untouchable."

"Interesting."

"What? That cops abuse their power or that I realize it?"

"Your position on it all. It's interesting."

"Really? Do you think they're in the right when they do that shit?"

He shook his head. "I don't care much for 'em, either."

I sighed in relief. "Good. I thought we were going to have to throw down."

He chuckled. "So now you want to fight me?"

"I would."

"If I said I liked cops?"

"No," I said. "If you said they were in the right."

He nodded and reached for his chopsticks.

The restaurant we were in was huge, and probably had seating for 200 people. At three-fourths capacity, they were busy, but not packed. As Dick ate his noodles and I sipped my broth, I gazed at the eclectic mix of patrons.

I noticed a man walk in who was wearing a robe. At first, he reminded me of Drake. The guy with him was rocking a ridiculous mustache, but no beard. I personally found mustaches to be grotesque, and for that reason alone, he caught my attention.

As I was preparing to tell Dick about the man in the robe reminding me of Drake, he turned to face me and sat down.

It *was* Drake.

"Holy shit," I whispered. "Guess who just came in?"

He shrugged. "A bunch of cops?"

"No," I snapped back. "That lunchmeat eating friend of yours, Drake."

Clearly surprised, he craned his neck to see. "Where?"

"Over your left shoulder," I said. "Just sat down with some dude with a mustache. And he's wearing a fucking robe. Drake, not the dude with the 'stache."

He peered over his shoulder. "He always wears a robe."

A few seconds later, a really tall Asian man with terrible acne walked over to their table, sat down, and began to talk.

Dick spun around. "Grab your purse. Let's go."

"We're leaving?"

"Kind of," he said. "Follow me."

He tossed fifty bucks on the table, grabbed my hand, and quickly walked toward the back of the restaurant. We ducked behind a wall that separated the bathrooms from the dining area and followed it into the kitchen.

While people appeared to be surprised, no one seemed to really care that we barged through the kitchen. Feeling like I was involved in something much bigger than I probably was, my heart raced and my mind jumped to all kinds of conclusions of what was going on.

I imagined the man with the mustache was an undercover cop, because almost all cops that were undercover had a nasty fucking mustache to assist in their disguise. I figured the Asian man was Duc, the man Drake sent Dick to meet on the day we hid the Ferrari in his garage.

We burst through the back door and into a dirt parking lot filled with what I guessed were the employee's cars.

"What the fuck's going on?" I asked, knowing he wasn't going to tell me a thing.

"Give me a minute," he said.

He stared down at my feet for a moment and then looked up. "The other day, when I got hit, someone took something from me. Something expensive. I think the Asian guy might be the guy, but I got hit from behind, so I don't know."

"Go kick his ass and take it back."

I wanted to see Dick kick the shit out of someone, and it seemed like the most logical answer to his concern.

"It's not that easy. I took it from him in the first place."

I shook my head. "You stole it from the Asian guy?"

"Not exactly. I paid for it. But…" He inhaled a deep breath, held it for a moment, and then sighed. "Never mind."

*Shit! I wanted to hear the details.*

"So, what are we going to do?"

"Come on," he said. "We're going to the car. I need to think."

We walked around the restaurant, to his car, and then drove right back to the dirt parking lot we were previously standing in. The building sat on a corner, and the place where we were sitting allowed us to see most of the cars that were parked on the street. While we sat in the dark and stared at the parked cars, he began to explain things.

"I don't know why, but I like you," he said.

I could list all the reasons I liked him, but my guess was he really didn't want to know. I opted to go with the condensed version. "I like you too."

"I'm a thief," he said.

I played it cool. "Okay."

He stared out into the street, seemingly preoccupied with the parked cars. "I take shit. Big shit. From big people."

I acted unimpressed. "Okay."

"I take most of what I steal, turn it into non-traceable funds, and give most of it to people who need it."

He may have been a modern day Robin Hood in his own mind, but based on what his home and cars looked like, he didn't give it all to the needy. Not even close. I decided to use one of his own words to describe my thoughts.

"Interesting."

He turned toward me and glared. "Interesting? That's all you've got to say?"

"It's not real tough to figure out that you're into shady shit, Dude. I mean, really. I've known you for a week, and we've ran from the cops, you left me at some guy's house who has his own fucking casino – while you did a *delivery and a pick-up* – and then, two days later, you come to pick me up for a date and you've got a huge gash on your face. Oh, and the day we met, you were threatening to sell a guy's wife to the drug cartel. Yeah, I think *interesting* is a pretty accurate statement."

"So what do you think?"

What did I think? I thought he was sexy. I liked the thought of him being a criminal. I wasn't ready to tell him that just yet, so I shrugged. "About what?"

"About what I told you."

"I'm here, aren't I?"

"Will I see you again? I guess that's the question."

I didn't get my point across. Maybe it was because I was too busy being a smart ass. We had gone from having a few random sexual encounters to him opening up to me, and I was really excited that he was. I often had a difficult time conveying my feelings and I found it no surprise that he was confused regarding what I was feeling or thinking.

I turned in my seat to face him. "I like you. I liked you the day we met. I like bad boys. Criminals. Tough guys. Whatever you want to call them. I just have really bad luck in relationships. Maybe it's my mouth, I don't know. But that day we ran from the cops? That's the most fun I've had in a long, long time. So, am I okay with you stealing big shit from big people? Yeah, I really am." I paused for effect and then continued. "Do you need an accomplice? A partner?"

He chuckled. "No."

"You sure?"

He laughed again. "Quite."

"This stuff is exciting," I said.

"What stuff?"

I waved my hands toward the street. "This."

"Oh shit," I whispered. "It's the Asian guy and that creepy ass Drake."

Dick turned and looked out the windshield. As the two men stood beside a white car and talked, he clenched his jaw and breathed through his nose.

"I wonder where the guy with the mustache went?" I whispered.

"What guy with a mustache?"

The guy that was with Drake," I said.

"I didn't see him. What'd he look like?"

"Like a guy with a mustache. I don't know, they all seem to look the same. They creep me out."

He glared.

"He was just kinda short and gross."

Drake turned away. The Asian guy got in the white car and drove off.

"Are we going to follow him?" I asked excitedly.

"No," he said.

"Why not?"

"It doesn't matter. I wanted to see if they were doing a deal. It doesn't look like it."

"Maybe they did it inside."

"Possible, but I doubt it," he said.

A few seconds later, Drake's Corvette drove by.

Dick sighed. "Ready?"

When he asked, I couldn't help but laugh to myself and wonder just what was going to happen next.

"Yep."

# TWELVE

# DICK

**MOST** who met me wanted me for what they perceived to be my wealth. I had no real friends, other than the few associates I had developed through my criminal activities.

Jess was different. She was with me because she enjoyed my company. It was nice for once to have someone appreciate me for who I was and not what I had.

"So just what is it that you find attractive about me?"

She glanced around my living room. "Truth or a lie?"

"Truth."

"Your big dick."

I laughed. "Yeah, right."

"It's true," she said. "That's the main reason."

"You're with me because I have a big dick?"

"Yep."

I stood up and walked to the kitchen. "I'm trying to be serious."

"I *am* being serious. You asked for the truth, I gave it," she said.

I grabbed another beer from the refrigerator. "So I've got a big cock and no other redeeming qualities?"

"You've got a few others, but I'm trying to look past everything else," she said.

"Why?"

"Because I don't know what's gonna happen next. For right now, you're just a big dick."

"Are you fucking serious?"

She nodded. "Dead serious."

I sat down across from her and studied her. She wasn't smiling. "So why are you here?"

"It feels really good when you fuck me. Like, *really* good."

"You're serious?"

"Uh huh."

"What if I had a little cock. Like half the size of what I've got?"

"A dick half the size of yours is still a pretty good size." She shrugged. "I'd probably still be here."

She was starting to piss me off. "God damn it. Okay, what if I had a really small cock. Would you be here?"

"Like, right now?"

"Yeah. Would you be here, right now, talking to me?"

She shook her head. "Nope."

"You're here strictly for the dick?"

"Pretty much. I mean, you're cool and stuff, but you're not interested in anything but fucking, so I'd be a fool to get all caught up in who you are. Dudes like you dump chicks like me. And, the last I heard, all I was entitled to was a one-night stand."

I glared at her.

She raised her index finger. "Oh, wait. I guess, technically, that day you fucked me in the ass in the parking lot at Target, you said I was *alright*. So, I've got that going for me."

"I'm not saying I do, but if I wanted more from you. If this wasn't just us fucking, what would you say my redeeming qualities are?"

"If we were just talking? Like just kicking it?" she giggled. "Hanging out and being besties?"

"Yeah."

"Well," she said. "I like it that you're demanding. And that you're really confident. I like the way you walk. And how you carry yourself. You know, your swagga."

"My swagger?"

She shook her head. "Swagga."

"Swagga."

"Yep. I like it," she said. "And how you're a prick. I like that. It's hot."

I set my beer on the end table and folded my arms in front of my chest. "A prick, huh?"

"Uh huh."

"Give me a for instance."

"Well, like when we went out the first time and you said 'grab your purse, we're leaving and I'm gonna make sure your mouth is too full to talk later' or whatever you said. I liked that. It was a total dick move for you to act like that, but it made me wet. I loved it."

I had no idea. I narrowed my eyes and stared at her. "Ready?"

She shrugged. "Sure."

"Stand up," I demanded.

"What?"

With my arms still folded in front of my chest, I stood up, glared at her, and cleared my throat. "Stand. Up."

She stood up.

I took a step toward her. "Get on your knees," I said dryly.

She lowered herself to her knees.

I took another step in her direction, unzipped my zipper, and pulled out my cock. "Open your mouth."

She opened her mouth.

I stopped. She met my gaze.

I stroked my cock a few times. She seemed to be waiting on instructions. "Is that a turn on?" I asked.

"Huh?"

"Is that a turn on?"

Her eyes fell to my cock. "Uh huh."

I walked back to the loveseat and sat down.

"What are you doing?" she snarled.

"I was just seeing something."

"Seriously?" she snapped back. "What, seeing if I was human?"

"No, seeing if you liked it when I acted like that."

"Fuck yeah, I do."

"I had no idea. I've always acted like that because I thought it'd keep people away, not attract them."

"So it's an act?" she huffed. "You're not really like that?"

"No, I'm pretty much just like that. It's difficult for me to be otherwise, but I can be polite if I need to be. I never knew anyone liked it, though. I think you're a first."

"Well," she said. "Most girls probably don't dig it, but I do. I love guys who are dicks. If a guy can talk a mad line of shit to me, he'll win my heart quicker than a guy with flowers."

"No shit?"

"No shit."

"Interesting," I said.

"Why'd I know you were going to say that?" She pressed her biceps into the sides of her breasts and shot me a seductive look. "So should I get up off my knees, or are you going to feed me that big cock?"

"No, get up. We're just talking for now."

She pressed her palms onto the floor and braced herself as she stood. "Asshole."

I nodded. "That's what I hear."

She sat down and reached for her glass of wine. "So, what about that goofy fucking Drake? That weirdo was eating rotten bologna and did you see he was eating a nasty fucking wiener when we got there?"

"What about him?"

"He's fucking weird. Wearing a robe out to eat and shit. Is that the types of friends you have?"

"He's an associate."

She took a drink of wine. "Do you have any friends?"

"Some."

"Are they like him?"

"No one's like Drake."

"True that," she said with a laugh.

I sat and studied her for a long moment as she drank her wine. After a few minutes, she broke the silence.

"So if we're just fucking, and that's it – an extended one-night stand or whatever – why am I here? Like right now?"

I raised my beer bottle and tipped it toward her. "That's a damned good question."

# THIRTEEN

# JESS

I thought I'd had a few big cocks in my day. Then Dick fucked me. From that point on, all previous dicks became faint memories.

Unimportant.

When I really thought about it, being with him because he was hung seemed ridiculous. Then, he'd fuck me again, and remind me what was so perfect about being completely filled with cock. And, the difference between being fucked and being filled was vast.

I liked Dick. A lot. A combination of his criminal behavior and his natural ability to be an asshole attracted me to him, but it was his big fat dick that sealed the deal.

I felt like a tramp.

A really satisfied tramp.

"So, what's the deal with that guy from the other night?" Katie asked.

"Nothing."

"What'd you guys do?"

"Nothing."

"Since when did you go out with a guy and not have a story to tell? Something's up."

"We just went out to eat and then hung out at his place."

She looked at me like I was speaking Latin. "You didn't bone?"

"Yeah, we boned."

She glanced around the empty bar. "And since then, you've taken off like four nights. Early. You've been with him, haven't you?"

"Uh huh."

"What the fuck, Jess? Let's hear it."

I was sure Dick wouldn't like it if I told anyone about who he really was, but hiding the facts about his big dick just seemed senseless. To experience something as magical as Dick's dick – and not share it with the world – was ridiculous.

"Let me ask you something. Have you ever been with a guy who has a really, really and I mean *really* big dick?"

"Roe had a big dick. It was huge."

"The mixed dude you were seeing last summer?"

"Uh huh. God, I swear, his dick was so big. That guy could make me come in about three strokes. And then. Over and over. It was crazy."

I didn't care about Roe. Or his dick. I wanted to tell her about Dick. "Compare it to something," I said.

"Uhhm. I dunno. Like Have you ever had a threesome? And like had one in your butt and your hoo-hah at the same time? It was like that. Only it was like that every time he fucked me."

I laughed so hard it started a coughing fit. Katie was a ditz. The fact that she compared it to being pounded by two dicks at once – and called her twat a hoo-hah – was another reason to laugh altogether.

She wrinkled her nose. "What?"

"You dork. I meant compare his dick to something. Like an object. And what the fuck with the DP? You're a freak."

"Oh." She laughed. "Yeah, Roe was into all kinds of stuff."

"So, compare the weirdo's cock to something."

"Uhhm. Like, maybe, I dunno. Like those sausages. The big ones. Bratwurst. Yeah, like a bratwurst."

"Bratwurst dick?"

"Uh huh." She nodded. "Just like that."

"Lemme see your arm." I said.

I was what most would describe as curvy, but I wasn't a big girl. Katie was a skinny meth-head looking bitch. She didn't do drugs, but she could pass for a coke whore for sure. She was five foot three and weighed all of 100 pounds if she was dressed in a parka.

"From your elbow to where your hand starts, and a little thicker than that skinny little wrist of yours. Ten fucking inches, bitch."

She slapped her hand against my shoulder. "Get out of here."

"Quit fucking hittin' me," I said. "And yeah, I'm serious."

"His dick's as big as my arm?"

"Uh huh. No shit. Ten thick inches of it."

I liked saying it.

*Ten inches.*

"Holy crap. So being fucked by him is like being fisted?"

"You're gross. Did Roe do that shit, too?"

"Uh huh."

"That's nasty."

"It feels so good," she said.

"If it feels like Dick's dick, yeah, I'll give you that. But I'm not looking to have a guy shove his hand up my puss."

She shrugged. "So, what's he like?"

"He's a prick. A complete asshole. But I like him."

"Assholes are the best. Well. Some of them," she said. "The good kind of asshole, or the bad kind?

I had an idea of what she was talking about, but I wanted to hear it from her. "What's the difference?"

"The good ones are just dicks. The bad ones are mean and slap you around or punch your face. I like good assholes, they make me feel loved."

It made perfect sense.

To me.

I felt the exact same way. A guy ordering me around and telling me what to do, then talking shit to me when he wasn't happy with me made me feel like he cared, as senseless as it sounded. "I agree totally."

She sighed. "I need a guy like that."

I grinned. Talking to her about him made me feel like whatever I had with Dick was significant, although I really knew it wasn't. In the end, I was a chick he was banging. For the time being, I'd live with it. I was just happy he opened up to me and that I was able to see him more than the one time he initially agreed to.

"Is he into freaky shit?"

"I dunno." I shrugged. "I stood outside the car and he shoved my head in the seat and butt fucked me in Target's parking lot off of I-35 the other day. In broad daylight."

"Cool," she said as if it were no big deal. "Is he, like, into threesomes?"

I had no idea, but I answered anyway. "Uhhm. No."

If he was, Katie wouldn't be the chick I'd choose for our third. It'd have to be a bitch with some meat on her bones. Someone worth losing my threesome virginity to. Not some skinny bitch that only wanted my man's cock. Or fist. It'd have to be a bad bitch.

Like Nicki Minaj.

I'd let Nicki Minaj stick her tongue in my ass while Dick was balling me for sure.

"Let me ask you something," I said.

"Okay."

"Do you like it in the butt?"

"Uh huh."

"Okay, when you're you know, when your guy starts off, does it send a freaking shockwave through you and make you just lose it?"

"Like make me come?"

"Uh huh."

"Yeah. It's pretty good stuff, why?"

"I dunno. I think I have some fascination with getting poked in the butt." I chuckled. "It makes me come so hard."

"Well, graduate to getting two at once," she said. "That? That's as close to heaven as you'll ever be."

"He poked his finger in my butt while he was fucking me on Wednesday. So, that was pretty close."

She shook her head and laughed. "It's not the same."

"What you fucking girls doing? I fucking fuck. Standing for the ever. Why no work? Your ethics is for shit. Fucking fuck," Patel complained.

I glanced at the clock. "It's ten till. We're not open yet."

He shook his head. "I fucking swearing."

I shrugged. "Ten minutes is ten minutes."

"And ten inches is ten inches," Katie whispered.

"Amen sista."

Patel looked up from the liquor ledger. "I swear to fuck. I should sell this bitch."

*Do us all a favor, fucktard.*

"I'll go open up," Katie said.

"Fine with me. Hell, yesterday I made $25 bucks over the lunch rush."

She laughed. "Thirty. But I had a big tipper."

The instant she unlocked the door, it swung open.

*Dick.*

He was dressed in navy slacks, a white button-down shirt, and a black jacket. He looked like he was preparing for a photoshoot for GQ Magazine. I grinned and gave a silly wave, and then realized the only reason he would come in would be to see me.

I really liked looking at him.

"Hi," Katie said, almost giggling as she said it. "Jess is over there."

"Thanks," he said.

"Hey," I said.

"Son of bitch. Mr. Dick," Patel shouted. "Patron?"

Dick waved. "No, just here to talk to Jess for a minute."

Patel ran over and shook Dick's hand like they were long lost buddies. "Nice to see you, Bro."

*Bro?*

Dick patted him on the shoulder and stepped to the side. "I'll holler at you before I go."

"Right on," Patel responded.

*Right on? Seriously?*

*You fucking phony motherfucker.*

"What are you doing tonight?" he asked.

"Working. Why?"

"Fuck. Can you get off?"

"I can, I'm sure. I had the early shift today. I normally don't work 'till 3:00, but today I had the 11:00 to 7:00. What time are you talking?"

"I don't know, like maybe 5:00. It'll give us time to rehearse everything."

*Rehearse?*

"Huh? What's going on?"

"I need you to do something for me. You wanted to know if I needed a partner, right?"

*Holy shit. Being involved in criminal activities. My dream come true.*

I nodded like a fat kid who'd been asked if he wanted another piece of pie. "Uh huh."

His mouth did the smirk thing it always did. "Well, I still don't. But. I could use some serious help tonight. It'll take two hours, maybe a little longer. And you'll have to lie and make it sound convincing."

It sounded mysterious. "Okay."

"I'll pay you a grand."

I could sure use the money, but I couldn't take it from him. "I don't want your money."

He waved me off. "What size shoes you wear?"

"Eight."

"And that dress the other night. What was it, a six?"

"Uh huh."

"Bra?"

"What about it?"

He gave me a shitty glare. "Size?"

"Oh. Depends. In the Victoria's Secret Bombshell, a 34D."

If he was going shopping for me, I so wanted him to get me one of those bras. At $75 a pop, my lingerie drawer was void of such luxuries.

"What are you doing?" I asked.

"I'll have some clothes for you. You're sure 5:00 will work?"

113

"I'll make it work. I'll get someone to come in early."

"Alright. I've got some shit to do," he said. "See you at 5:00. I'll just pick you up here."

I grinned. "Okay."

"See you then."

"Hey, you told Patel you were gonna…"

He glanced over his shoulder. "Patel's an asshole."

One more reason I liked Dick.

"That, he is."

He reached for the door and turned around. "See you at 5:00."

# FOURTEEN

## DICK

"**SO**, the day I made the pickup and the delivery for Drake, I called him. I made him think I was already there – ready to do the drop-off – and that Duc's guys were waiting to receive the package."

"Okay," Jess said.

"But I wasn't. I looked in the case to see what I was delivering, and it was a huge fucking diamond. $3,000,000 worth of diamond. And Drake said he was selling it for a $1,000,000. So, I came home, got $1,000,000, kept the diamond, and gave my money to Drake. Unless he heard otherwise, he'd assume the money came from Duc."

I'd picked Jess up from work and we were sitting in my living room going over my plan. She sat on the couch across from me, and I sat beside the clothes I'd purchased for her on the loveseat. It seemed strange trusting her – because I trusted no one – but after her performance during the car chase with the cops, trusting her seemed to come pretty easy.

Her eyes widened. "Duc's the guy from the noodle place? With Drake?"

I nodded. "That's him."

"This is so exciting."

"I'm not done yet."

"Sorry."

"So, I took the diamond to a buyer. There's only a few guys in town that'll buy a stone like that, and I took it to one who I've dealt with in the past. He offered me $3,000,000, which would make me $2,000,000 profit. He needed a few days to get the money from investors, so I took the stone and left. On my way to the car…"

I pointed to the gash on the top of my head. "Some fucker smacked me. When I woke up, no diamond."

"No honor amongst thieves," she said.

"Exactly."

"So what were you going to do when Duc said he never got it. That you didn't deliver it?"

"He'd tell Drake. Drake would call me, and I'd tell him that one of Duc's crew paid me for it. The phone call I made to him from Chinatown with all the gooks chatting in the background would support it."

She looked confused. "But then they'd just say they didn't get it. That you were lying."

"And I'd say they did. Drake would believe me. And Duc would question his guys because he doesn't trust anyone. It'd start a war within his little crew, and I hate that fucker."

"Wouldn't Drake just assume you did what you did?"

I shook my head. "No one thinks I've got that kind of liquid cash."

"It's crazy that you do."

I shrugged. "Gotta have money to make money."

"So, now what?"

I raised my index finger. "I'm getting to that. What do you know about diamonds?"

She spread her fingers apart and turned the backs of her hands toward me. "Do I look like I know anything about diamonds?"

"I'll give you a quick lesson in a minute. Here's what we're going to do. You're going to get dressed up and become a rich single widow. You're going to be 30, and your husband, who was 50, died last year of a heart attack. Now, a year later, your diamond ring was misplaced and then stolen while you were getting a massage. When you got home and realized you didn't have it, you called the parlor, and it wasn't there. Whatever. Make something up. But you're looking for a replacement ring. Your husband was some oil tycoon, and money's no object. All you really care about is the size. And you want a big one."

"So who am I buying this diamond from? Not Duc?" she asked.

"No. You're going to the jeweler who I tried to sell it to. Anyone around here who wants to turn that thing to cash will go to him. He'll know where it is, or he should. But if Duc has it, the jeweler won't tell me. But he'll get ahold of it for you."

"This is so exciting. I gotta pee."

I chuckled. "You know where it is."

While she walked away, I admired the dress I purchased. Jess always looked good, but she was going to look great wearing everything I had picked out for her. As she walked back into the room I acted disinterested in the clothes and sat down.

She plopped down on the couch and chuckled. "Okay. Where we left off. I want a big one. How ironic is that?"

"Stop it," I said.

She let out a sigh. "Okay," she said innocently.

"So, when it comes to diamonds, there are a few things that are important. The four C's. Color, cut, clarity, and carat weight. Color is just that, the color of the diamond. They range from black to colorless. Cut is the manner in which the stone is cut. The depth, width, how the facets align with everything. How it reflects light. Clarity is how clear the diamond is of flaws. It could be a great color, and have specs of carbon in it, making its clarity a poor grade. And carat weight is the size. Following me so far?"

"Color, cut, clarity, carat weight," she said.

"Impressive."

"I'm a good listener."

"If you go in this place and ask for exactly what I'm looking for, it's going to look pretty obvious. What I had was a flawless ten carat round colorless stone. You're going to say yours was a six carat *cushion* cut, which is a square cut with the corners cut off. And you know your husband told you it was flawless and he got it in Houston, not here. If you say he bought it here, he'll ask too many questions."

"I can do this."

"I know you can. We'll go over it some more, just so you're comfortable. Hopefully, if you press him hard enough, he'll offer the other stone up for sale. Just remember, price is no object."

"Okay."

"Now, the clothes. I bought a dress, shoes, and I have some jewelry for you to wear. And when you go, you'll take the Maserati."

"What's a Maserati?"

I laughed. "It's a car. An expensive car."

"Did you get the bra? The Bombshell?"

"Actually, I got a few of them. I wasn't sure about which color to get."

"Sweet."

I stood up and motioned toward the clothes. "So, you're going to need to take this stuff and try it on."

"I'll just try them on here," she said.

She stood and quickly pulled her tee shirt over her head. After tossing her shoes to the side, she pushed her shorts down her tanned legs and kicked them to the side. Now standing in front of me in her bra and panties, she looked remarkably young and innocent.

Yet she was neither.

She reached back, unclasped her bra, and allowed it to fall down along her arms. As it dropped to the floor, I felt myself growing stiff.

"We haven't got time for this," I said. "You need to be there no later than 6:00. It's 5:30 now."

She pressed her thumbs under the sides of her panties. "No time for what?"

I pushed the heel of my palm against my cock, attempting to situate it in my slacks. "For you fucking with me."

She pushed her panties down along her thighs, making eye contact with me the entire time.

Her little charade worked. I was pitching a tent in my slacks. "We haven't got time, Jess," I said sternly.

She lifted her panties with her toe, extended her leg to the side, and flicked them on top of the pile of clothes. "Okay."

Completely naked, she walked toward me, carefully placing one foot directly in front of the other as if she were walking down a runway in a fashion show.

"Did you get me any panties?"

I shook my head.

"Shame," she said. "I'll have to go commando. I hope he doesn't get a glimpse of my cooter."

She stopped a few feet from me, turned around completely, and bend at the waist. Hovering over the pile of clothes with her ass pointed directly at my face, she admired the dress.

"This is pretty."

I stared at her pussy. I pressed my tongue against the roof of my dry mouth and fought to swallow. "Uh huh."

"It's so soft and smooth."

Although she couldn't see me, I nodded in agreement.

She glanced over her shoulder. "I like how it feels when I touch it."

I twisted to the side and pressed down against my stiff cock. "You little bitch. Do you think you can manipulate me into giving you some dick?"

She straightened her posture and turned to face me. "All this talk about stealing and trying to get the diamond back made my little pussy wet." She reached down, cupped her hand against her crotch, and curled her middle finger upward.

"It just slipped right in there. Did you see that?" She raised her free hand to her mouth and covered it, feigning innocent shock.

If her ability to act when she was in front of the jeweler was no better than what I was seeing, I'd never find out where my diamond was.

I knew there was no time for sex, but my stiff dick didn't seem to care about my schedule. "Get dressed." I snapped.

"Fine," she said. "Maybe I'll get that jeweler guy to give me some dick."

I glared at her. "The fuck you will."

She picked up the dress. "I'm dripping wet. I don't want it, I *need* it. I bet if I ask him really nice, he'd take me in the back and give me some. I might even find out where your diamond is."

The thought of it infuriated me. I unbuckled my belt, unzipped my slacks, and pushed them to mid-thigh.

"If there's going to be any dick given to you, it comes from me. Understand?" I snarled.

A shocked look washed over her and she swallowed heavily. "Now? Or, uhhm, always?"

"Until I say differently," I said. "Now, bend the fuck over."

She pressed her bare chest onto the loveseat. I gripped my cock in my hand, and with my slacks around my thighs, stumbled toward her.

I stood behind her for a moment, admiring her. The late-evening sun came through the large windows on the western wall, and provided natural lighting for the entire room. Seeing her bent over and ready to give herself to me sexually was a beautiful sight. Her skin seemed to have more radiance, a deeper color – a certain glow I had yet to notice.

Astonished at what was before me, I stood in complete awe and stared.

Something had changed.

I shook my head and guided my stiff cock into her tight warmth. It felt heavenly to be inside of her; her tight pussy clenching me like a vise. I closed my eyes and sighed quietly as each stiff inch of my cock slipped inside.

She moaned in pleasure. I pushed my hips against her rounded butt cheeks, burying myself as deep within her as I possibly could. With my balls against her clit, and the head of my dick bottomed out deep in her vaginal walls, I leaned forward and pressed my lips to her ear.

"Until further notice, this little pussy of yours is mine. No one else's. Mine."

"Ohh...Kay," she breathed.

I lifted my mouth from her ear, pulled my cock halfway out, and shoved it back inside of her completely.

"Say it!"

"Uhhm." She grunted. "Yours."

"Each time it bottoms out, Jess. Each time. Tell me whose little pussy this is."

I pulled out, closed my eyes, and slowly slid myself in until I hit bottom.

"Yours," she bellowed.

I cleared my throat. "My what?"

"Your pussy."

I had no idea if there was a heaven, and if there was I doubted I was going to receive a formal invitation to reside there when my life was over.

But if there was a heaven on earth, there was no doubt I had found it. And I was ten inches deep in it.

I gripped her waist in my hands, gazed down, and followed the curve of her back until my eyes were fixed on her little round ass.

I inhaled a deep breath and began to pound my way into her long-term memory.

"Your pussy."

"Your...pussy."

I watched my long thick shaft slide in and out of her tightness with each stroke. Seeing it disappear deep inside of her was a satisfying sight.

"Your. Fucking. Pussy."

"Your pussy."

"Your...Oh fuck."

"Yes. Fuck it. It's yours. Oh..."

The sound of our bodies slapping together filled the silent space between her screams. I felt my balls tighten.

"Your pussy."

I continued to fuck her without reservation.

I stared down at her in wonder of what I had done in my life to be so deserving. I decided it was a fluke. A mistake. An accident. Some strange coincidence that brought us together, and eventually she would be taken from me.

Because I wasn't worthy of such beauty.

"Your fucking pussy," she grunted.

I could feel myself reaching climax. I reached around her waist with the intention of fingering her clit, only to find her hand between her legs doing just that. I wiped my index finger alongside her cock-filled pussy and soaked it with her juices.

She seemed to enjoy ass play, so I pushed my finger into her tight ass.

"Oh fuck yes," she wailed. "That's yours too."

I felt her pussy contract. In response, I buried myself deep while I fingered her ass gently. Together, we reached climax. My balls felt like they exploded, and my mind went along with them, leaving me standing there a mindless vessel filled with emotion.

At that moment, my only concern was that she was happy. Nothing else mattered. Not diamonds. Or money. Not even Asian drug lords.

Yet.

I knew there was no way I could share with her how I felt.

# FIFTEEN

# JESS

**HE** was bald, short, and had a kidney-shaped mole on his chin the size of a dime. With eyes that were filled with excitement and a tone of voice that came close to matching, he explained the dilemma. "A gem like the one you're describing won't come easy. Did your husband give you any indication of what he paid for the one that was lost?"

His transparent short-sleeved polyester shirt had two wet spots beneath his arm pits, and another in the center of his hairy chest. Black and gray hair sprouted out of the top of his undershirt, which was easy to see through the opening created by the three buttons of his shirt he left unbuttoned.

"Oh, it wasn't lost. It was *stolen*. As sure as I'm standin' here." I glanced over each shoulder, squeezed my boobs together with my upper arms, and leaned forward as if telling him a secret.

With his beady little eyes fixed on my tits, he leaned forward.

I cupped my hand around the side of my mouth and pressed the back of my hand against the front of his ear.

"There were some Yankee women in the parlor. From back east. Philadelphia, I heard one say," I said, forcing my breath into his ear.

He gasped and stood straight up. "God damned Yankees. I'm sorry, but you can't trust 'em."

"Oh, believe me. I'm sure my poor Preston is turnin' over in his grave. I bet he is. Bless his soul."

"A diamond like you've described…" He sighed heavily and began to drum his fingers against the receiver of a phone that was sitting on the lower counter. "A difficult one to find."

I reached for the tennis bracelet Dick gave me to wear, and adjusted it on my wrist without looking, making it seem as natural as I could. "Now Preston didn't share such things with me, especially with it bein' a gift, but I do know we had it insured for $5,000,000 – but only if it was taken from the home. I've already called the underwriter. Now that's a thief for you. I tell you what, let me give you some free advice."

I folded my arms underneath my boobs and pressed them up as far as I could without causing them to fall out of the top of the bra. I leaned forward and his eyes fell to my chest. "I've got another secret for ya," I whispered.

With his eyes glued to my awesome cleavage, he bent over and rested his elbows against the glass display case.

"Read the fine print," I whispered. "Those insurance companies are the biggest thieves of them all."

"Isn't that the truth."

He stood, and I stayed leaning over the glass case, my boobs bubbling out of the new bra and free for him to eye fondle through plunging neckline of the dress.

His eyes shifted back and forth between my tits and my eyes. "A cushion cut, was it?"

I blinked a few times. "Yes, Sir, it was. Five carats."

"And you're wanting an exact replacement?"

"Nothin' in life is exact, is it?" I chuckled. "Now with my blessed

Preston gone, I suppose I could go a little larger. In his memory, of course. Back when he got the ring, oil was down at $33 a barrel. Right after he passed, it was just under $100. I sold the field in Harris County right after he…"

Without standing, I paused and wiped my eyes. "I think he'd want me to go a little bigger. And I've always said bigger's better. Preston would just laugh when I did. He had a sense of humor like that. Laughin' at my jokes, you know?"

He grinned and nodded. "With diamonds and a few other things, bigger *is* better."

"Oh, let me tell you how we met," I interrupted. "That darned Maserati Preston bought me. I'd just as soon have me a big ol' pickup truck. Bigger is better when it comes to vehicles, and that's a fact. A big truck just makes me grin from ear to ear. You see, I grew up dirt poor. We had us a trailer house outside of Tomball, Texas, and my daddy told me I'd never amount to a hill of beans. I knew better. I didn't tell my daddy, because there's some things you just don't tell your daddy, but…"

I glanced over each shoulder and bent over the counter again.

Baldie leaned forward, locked eyes with my tits, and grinned.

"I could suck a golf ball through a garden hose, and swallow an axe handle without gaggin'. That's how I met Preston. I was dancing at the Pink Taco right off of 249 and Spring-Canyon Road, and in he came. He wanted him a lap dance, but I saw that watch he was wearin' and I just said what the heck."

I stood up and grinned. "You ever said that? What the heck?"

He swallowed hard. A nod of his head followed.

"Oh my." I fanned my hand in front of my face. "It's downright warm in here."

"It sure is."

"Now what about my little diamond? I'd sure like to have it before Preston's birthday. It'd be nice to have it when I go out to dust his headstone."

"When might that be?"

"The 21st. In thirteen days."

Dick and I hadn't discussed a time frame, and the idea of using my dead husband's birthday as a deadline just came to me. After I spoke, I hoped the date would work for all parties involved.

His face was red and he was covered in beads of sweat. He rubbed his palm over the top of his bald head, returned a wet hand, and wiped it against his thigh. "Let me step in the back, and check my ledger. I may be able to help you; I'll just need to check. I'll be right back."

"Take your time," I said.

I wished Dick was there so he could see how well I was doing with the creepy little jeweler. I could tell he was talking to someone, and although I couldn't hear what he was saying clearly, I imagined the man with the mustache from the noodle place being on the other end of the phone. I felt that mustaches were the creepiest things ever, and believed the men who wore them were never honest, and only creeps. I threw up in mouth a little bit just as the Danny DeVito look-alike was returning.

"I'm afraid I have good news and bad news,' he said.

"The bad first. I love ending on a good note."

"I may be able to help you, but it's going to be twice the size of the original stone, and it will cost $4,000,000. It's a bargain at that price."

I stood there with a smile on my face and stared as if he hadn't spoken. He cleared his throat.

I chuckled. "Oh, I'm sorry. I was waiting for the bad news."

"That was the bad news."

"Oh, well, what's the good news?"

"I think we can get it by Preston's birthday, we'll just have to have the payment in cash or bank approved funds."

"That won't be a problem. Now, I have a friend who advises me in such matters, will he be able to inspect the diamond before I purchase it?"

"Certainly," he said. "Did I say the stone is round?"

"You didn't. I'm just so excited to get it replaced, I'm afraid the shape doesn't matter. How do we go proceed from here?"

"I'll need a way to contact you," he said. "And I'll be in touch."

The thought of giving the sweaty little man my phone number didn't appeal much to me, but I realized I had no choice.

I gave him my number, a huge grin, and another shot at my tits, then left.

I knew Dick would be happy with what I found out, but I wanted more. I needed to know who had the diamond.

And my bet was it was the man with the mustache.

# SIXTEEN

# DICK

**I'D** never really cared for anyone, at least not that I could remember. I was sure at one point in time I loved my parents, but I couldn't remember for the life of me when it was.

But Jess?

Jess was alright.

She gagged like she was going to barf. "I don't think I like it."

"You're not supposed to chew the fuckers like a piece of god damned gum. You just swallow them."

"Then why eat 'em? I mean, if you're just going to swallow 'em?"

We were in a restaurant eating oysters on the half shell as an appetizer while we waited for our meal. She tried to swallow the same one three times, and each time, it came right back up. Determined to succeed, she continued to try until she finally accomplished the task. Now, it was anyone's guess as to whether or not she'd keep it down.

She covered her hand with her mouth. "You can have the rest of 'em."

I chuckled. "You sure?"

She nodded.

I fixed my eyes on hers and slurped another from the shell slowly, exaggerating my slurping to irritate her.

She lunged forward, grabbed her stomach and coughed. The oyster shot from her mouth and landed on the plate in front of her.

She took a drink of water, glared at it, and picked it up.

"If you eat that nasty little fucker, you're going to make me barf," I said.

"I said I'd eat one, and I'm going to eat this little bastard."

"You've eaten that same one three times. This'll make four. That's gross."

She flattened her palm and stared down at the oyster. "I can't tell the difference between when I saw it on the shell, and now."

"Don't," I warned.

She lifted her hand, sucked the oyster into her mouth, and swallowed hard. After a few seconds she widened her eyes and opened her mouth. "Tadah!"

I pushed the plate to the side. "I'm done."

"There's like eight left, and you only bought twelve."

"I'm done."

"You think me eating that little fucker is gross?"

"I know it's gross," I said.

"And you want me to swallow your cum."

I shook my head. "That's different."

"How?"

"It's during the throes of passion or whatever."

"That first night? You stuck your big fat dick in me. I was drunk as fuck. You didn't know me. You were going to fuck me and forget me. You told me that. You said that's all anyone got from you. And then you stuck your finger in my ass."

"You told me to."

"I wasn't done." She chuckled. "Anyway. I came all over your big fat cock, collapsed, and flopped onto my knees and sucked you off. You came like a porn star. And I swallowed that shit. So what, you're going to tell me that was love?"

I shrugged. "No."

"Was it gross?" she asked.

"No."

"Okay, then why is me eating that oyster gross?"

"It just is."

"Swallowing cum is more gross."

"Why don't you barf it up?"

She took a drink of wine, cleared her throat, and leaned forward. "Do you think girls like swallowing cum? Do you think we like the taste?"

I shrugged. I hadn't really thought about it. As many of them did it, it would stand to reason that there was some redeeming quality about the taste. "I guess so."

"We don't. It's fucking gross. Its slippery, slimy, salty, and bitter. It's like rotten salty raw eggs."

The three oysters I had eaten were churning in my stomach. "Why do you do it?"

"The same reason every other girl does it. We want to make you happy. To satisfy you."

"But you don't like it?"

"Fuck no. But I like *doing* it."

"That makes no sense."

"Maybe not to you. But it does to me. Look at it this way. The night I met you I swallowed your spunk. I swallowed that shit and acted like

133

it was candy. Did that turn you on?"

I nodded. "Fuck yeah."

"Okay. And look at me now. I'm still here. I bet if I would have collapsed on the bed and fell asleep I wouldn't be."

"Probably not."

"Why?"

I shrugged. "I don't know. Because you lacked determination or something."

"And now you know why I tried four times to eat that raw fucking oyster."

"Why?" I asked.

"Because you wanted me to try it. And for the same reason I swallowed you cum, I was determined to swallow that grotesque little clam or whatever those fuckers are. I wanted you to be happy with me."

I considered her logic and eventually nodded. "I think it makes sense."

She laughed. "You think so?"

"I do."

She brushed her hair over her shoulder and grinned a shitty little grin. "Appreciate me a little more?"

I did. I never looked at things the way she presented them. I never had to. Now that she made her points, I did appreciate her more. It seemed to be something that was happening on a daily basis.

"I do."

"Good."

She took another drink of wine. "So, you say my pussy is yours. Is your cock mine?"

"No."

"Really?" She dragged the two syllables along for two really long seconds. "Why not?"

"I don't know. Guys don't do that shit. They don't say *this cock is yours*. And girls don't say shit like *whose cock's in me* or whatever."

"I want that big fucker to be mine."

"Why?"

She shrugged. "So I can say it's mine."

"Who would you tell?"

She acted like she really thought about it for a while. "Nobody, I guess. Just myself."

"So it'd be your cock, but you'd just keep it hush hush?"

"Sure."

"Okay, take it. It's yours."

She sat up in her seat. "Really?"

"Yep. It's yours, claim it."

"Are you saying that because you know I won't tell anybody, or because you really want me to have it? I don't want it if it's some wordplay bullshit. I want that fucker because I really like it. And I don't want anyone else to have it."

"Right now, I'm not considering giving it to anyone else."

"Right now while we're eating, or right now, like at this point in your life."

"The life thing, maybe. Long after dinner's over anyway." I chuckled. "Maybe even through the rest of the month."

She stared back at me. "No shit?"

I took a drink of my beer and nodded. "No shit."

"Fuck yes, that big fucker's mine." She reached for her wine. "I like you."

# DICK

"I like you back," I said.
And I meant it.

# SEVENTEEN

## JESS

**"WHERE** are we going?"

"I told you, we're going to meet someone. We need to see him before you try and buy that diamond back. I need to see if he knows anything."

I loved being linked to the underbelly of the city. The criminal side of things. It excited me to no end to *not* know what was going on with Dick and his illicit activities. I preferred formulating my own version in my head. In my mind we were solving mysteries and stealing for the betterment of mankind while the bad guys were one small step behind us.

And I loved it.

I imagined being captured, kidnapped, held hostage and slapped around. Not a lot. No broken teeth or bones, just a good hard slapping from some sweaty guy who had a dingy tee shirt, four day's growth of beard, and a beer belly. Dick would break the door down, kick the shit out of him just in time to save me, and we'd speed off in the Ferrari. Thinking about our criminal endeavors made me almost as wet as thinking about Dick's big dick.

Not knowing was killing me. "So who is this guy?"

He turned the corner and shot me a glare. "You'll see."

I wondered if it was Duc or Drake, but I doubted it. Duc looked scary at the restaurant, and Drake was just fucking weird. I really hoped it wasn't the guy with the creepy mustache, but I didn't think Dick knew who he was for sure, unless he found out and didn't tell me.

"It's not that creepy fucker with the mustache, is it?"

"Yeah, it's mustache man."

"Seriously?"

"No, it's not the guy with the mustache. I have no idea who that fucking guy is."

I released a sigh of frustration. Not a big one. But a necessary one. "Okay."

"When we go in here, don't stare at his scar," he said.

"He's got a scar?"

"A big one. On his neck. It goes from right below one ear almost to the other ear. It's pretty bad, just don't stare at it."

"Oh my God, what happened?"

"Guy tried to kill him. Cut his throat. Then, he crawled out into the street, and some lady almost fucking ran over him. She ended up taking him to the hospital. Saved his life."

The guy who got his throat cut probably didn't think so, but I thought it was an awesome story. "No shit?"

"No shit."

I often felt that I was more sensible than most people. "Why didn't she just call an ambulance."

"They were in Mexico."

"Oh."

"Just remember, no staring. Look past him. At the wall or something."

"Okay. I won't stare."

"He'll probably try to get you to get high, too. Just tell him you don't smoke."

"I don't."

"Tell him that. Be adamant."

It was almost dark, and we were driving through the hood. The neighborhood was a rundown area of Austin called Rundberg. Dick's Mercedes looked out of place amidst the shitty cars and shittier houses, and the farther we got into the neighborhood, the less I thought what we were doing was cool.

About the time I began to wonder about making it out alive, he pulled into a driveway and right beside one of the shitty little houses. It looked like at some point in time someone had started painting it, and then stopped. The front was yellow, and the back – and half the side – was gray. An old car was in the yard, but it had no wheels. Just the car, sitting down in the dirt.

There was a truck in the driveway in front of us, and I didn't need to ask if it ran, I could tell by looking at all of the shit leaned against it that it hadn't gone anywhere in a long, long time.

He put the car in park, shut off the engine, and looked at me. "Ready?"

I wasn't. I was scared. I nodded my head anyway. "Yep. Don't get high, and no staring."

"And don't go to the bathroom. I mean, not unless you have to."

I wrinkled my nose at the thought of what the shitty bathroom in the shitty two-tone house would look like and shook my head. "I should be fine as long as we're not staying."

"We're only staying as long as we have to."

I got out and paid close attention to where I walked to make sure I didn't step in anything I didn't want to. Dick checked over each shoulder and locked the car. I followed him to the door, and he knocked on it three times. And then two more.

*The secret knock.*

After a long wait, a man with a dingy shirt, a beer belly, and four day's growth of beard answered the door. My mouth flopped open. Immediately, I knew I did not want to be kidnapped or slapped around by him.

Not at all.

I couldn't tell for sure, but it looked like he was wearing boxer shorts. I tried to swallow, but apparently forgot how. I took a quick glance at his neck. A jagged scar followed right under his jaw from one side to another.

"Sorry, was in the crapper." He tossed his head toward me. "She cool?"

"She sure as fuck wouldn't be here if she wasn't, would she?"

The man eyed me for a minute, stepped to the side of the door, and nodded. "Come on in."

The inside of the home was remarkably neat and clean. I tried to make sense of why the yard, cars, and bathroom would be so disgusting – and the home so neat – but couldn't. I decided to listen to whatever he and Dick talked about and put the pieces of the puzzle together on my own.

I looked around the small living room. There was no couch. We all sat in separate chairs while the T.V. silently played a news station with a stock ticker at the top and bottom of the screen. The sweet smell of cinnamon lingered in the air.

Beer Belly shot me a glare, then quickly shifted his eyes to Dick. "So, your text was cryptic, as always. What's going on?"

"You turned me onto that deal with Fat Willie a couple of weeks ago. He just paid me."

Beer Belly reached for his neck. "Fat Willie who stays over in West Lake Oaks?"

I knew West Lake Oaks; it was a really ritzy neighborhood. I stared off to the side and acted disinterested, finding it odd that Dick didn't introduce me.

"There's only one Fat fucking Willie," Dick snapped

"I was just askin'."

"So, when you do a deal with Fat Willie, what stands out about him when he pays?"

"Pays in old bills and small bills, why?"

Out of my peripheral, I saw Beer Belly reach for his neck. Naturally, I wanted to see if he was scratching his scar, and I took a quick glance.

His eyes shot to me.

I looked away.

"Always. Not sometimes, always, right?" Dick asked.

I decided to listen to the conversation and try my luck at reading the lips of the guy on T.V.

"Always," Beer Belly agreed.

"Something's fucked up. He paid me $55,000 on a deal, and it was all $100's. New bills. Banded. No old bills, no small bills."

Beer Belly stood up. He *was* wearing boxer shorts. "Coffee?"

Dick shook his head. "No, I'm straight."

I continued to stare at the T. V. "Me too."

"What in the fuck does *me too* mean? One of us is getting' a cup, and one ain't. Me too yes or me too no?"

*Jesus.*

"No, thank you," I said.

"Suit yourself." He walked into the kitchen.

Dick glared at me. I shrugged and sniffed loudly. "What's with the cinnamon?" I whispered.

"It always smells like that in here."

I accepted his response, but I didn't like it. There had to be a reason. Beer Belly returned, eyeing me as he walked into the room.

I went back to reading lips.

Beer Belly sat down. "Odd he paid with new bills."

"I was thinking the same thing," Dick said.

"I'd ask him. Sounds like front money. Unless something's changed in his life, he's still spending all the money he made in the 1980's. Been spending it for a while. Strange thinking he's done spendin' it and he's dipped into a new stash."

"Yeah. Strange," Dick agreed.

"What the fuck is she doing?" Beer Belly asked.

I kept my eyes glued to the T.V.

"I don't know, ask her."

"Hey. What the fuck are you doing?"

"Trying to read this guy's lips," I said without looking away from the T.V.

He laughed. "You read lips, do you?"

"Not really."

"Maybe she's a cop," Beer Belly said.

*Fuck you and your cinnamon house.*

"She's not a cop."

"Maybe she's wearin' a wire."

*Are you serious?*

"She's not wearing a wire."

"Never know."

"I know."

"Oh really? You know, huh?"

Dick cleared his throat. "Don't care much for you accusing me of bringing a cop into your home."

*Thank you.*

"I wasn't accusing."

"You were, and you did. I brought her, she's cool."

"Fine. She's cool. Well, I'd ask Fat Willie where he got the cash. Straight up," Beer Belly said.

"I will. But that's not really why I'm here."

"I'm listenin'."

"What do you know about Drake getting his hands on a 10 carat stone?"

I glanced toward Beer Belly. His eyes shot wide as soon as Dick mentioned the diamond.

He reached for his neck. "Robe wearin' Drake?" he asked with a laugh. "I wouldn't have guessed it."

"Guessed what?" Dick snapped back.

"Didn't figure weird fuckin' Drake would ever end up with a rock like that. He don't know nothin' 'bout rocks."

"No arguments from me on that."

"Ain't seen that weird fucker in a spell," Beer Belly said. "When you see him last?"

"Couple of weeks ago. Needed to borrow a car."

"You see that 'Vette he bought?"

"As a matter of fact, he let me borrow it."

Beer Belly chuckled. "Must have needed a favor."

"Something like that," Dick responded. "I know you get a shot at every large rock that comes through this town, so what have you heard about the stone?"

Beer Belly took a drink of coffee and cleared his throat. "Dallas football player. Quarterback, if I remember right. Married some big titted country singer chick, and then caught her sucking off the place kicker. They split up, and she run off with the kicker. Quarterback ended up with some local chick wears cowboy hats all the time. Anyway, like all them fuckers do, he lived in one of those sprawlin' mansions. Well, him and cowgirl announced they was goin' to Hawaii to get hitched, and when they was gone, somebody broke in the home. Couldn't get the safe unlocked, so they just took the fucker. Said the safe weighed 1,600 pounds. Imagine haulin' that fucker out into the trunk of your Benz."

Dick shook his head. "Wouldn't happen."

"That's the only stone of that size I know about. It was the country music singer girl's wedding ring."

I'd seen the story he was talking about on the news. They didn't mention the diamond, but they did mention everything else.

"What do you know about the football player's stone?" Dick asked again.

Beer Belly adjusted himself in his seat. "Slightly over 10 carats. Round. Colorless. Flawless."

"Where would you price it? If you were guessing?"

"$3,650,000. And that ain't a guess. Been waitin' for it to come up for a while now, but ain't seen it yet."

"Heard anything about it?"

Beer Belly nodded. He took a sip of his coffee. "Asians. Rumor was they had it up for sale. I put a call in for it, but it disappeared."

"How long ago?" Dick asked.

"How long ago what?"

"How fucking long ago was it up for sale?"

"Couple weeks ago. In fact, I was gonna go give a bid on it, and then the fucker up and disappeared. Why so many questions?"

Dick shrugged. "Just curious. Heard a rumor a 10 carat rock was going out for bids and $1,000,000 was the price. Caught my interest, and then, like you said, it disappeared."

"Somebody's sellin' a rock like that for $1,000,000, they're either a cop or a dumbass."

"Agreed."

Beer Belly reached for his neck and rubbed his scar. "So you lookin' to buy it?"

Dick shook his head. "Just heard about it. Sounded too good to be true. Never been much of a dream chaser."

Beer Belly glared at me. "What the fuck are you lookin' at?"

*Shit.*

In all of the excitement of listening to the stories, I stopped reading lips and started paying attention. I wasn't staring, but I was following the conversation closely. In doing so, I ended up gazing blankly at Beer Belly.

"I uhhm…" I looked away.

He stood up. "You uhhm what? You lookin' at my fuckin' neck?"

I shook my head. "No."

"Sure as fuck was."

"Was not."

"Was too."

"Was not."

"Leave her alone. She wasn't looking at your neck."

Beer Belly glared at Dick. "How the fuck do you know?"

"I told her not to."

"You told her not to what? Not to look at my neck?"

Dick nodded.

"Why the fuck would you tell somebody that shit?" Beer Belly growled.

"Because you're sensitive about it. And you always end up doing this kind of shit when you think someone's looking at it."

"Fucker tried to cut off my head. You'd be sensitive about it too."

"Maybe you should wear a scarf," I said.

His eyes shot in my direction. "I knew you were fuckin' lookin'," he snarled.

The cinnamon. My full bladder. His weird scar. His awful attitude. It was too much. I snapped.

I stood up, crossed my arms, and fixed my eyes on his neck. "I wasn't fucking looking. I already saw it. I don't care anymore. Get fucking over yourself."

He started laughing. "Sure she ain't a cop?"

"She's not a cop," Dick said.

"Fuck you," I said. "You're a cop."

"Whoa!" he bellowed. "You don't go accusing people of shit like that unless…"

"Exactly," I interrupted. "How's it feel?"

He reached for his neck and covered it with his hand. "Don't say it again."

"You don't say it again," I snarled. "You and your fucking cinnamon house. Probably smells like this to hide the smell of pork, you fucking pig."

"Stop!" Dick shouted. He stood up and shook his head. "Jesus. Fucking. Christ. That's it, we're leaving. No more fighting, no more cop talk."

"Amen to that, Brother," Beer Belly said.

Dick nodded. "Appreciate your time, and I'll keep you posted if I hear anything."

"Don't bring your little tart with ya next time," Beer Belly said.

*Tart?*

I moved to Dick's side and turned around. "I'm not a fucking tart."

"Are too."

"Fuck you. Am not."

"Stop!" Dick shouted. "Jesus."

"Lemme know what you find out about Fat Willie. Anxious to find out what you find out about that money."

Dick opened the front door. "Will do."

While we were walking to the car, I thought of all the things about Beer Belly that I didn't like. His nervous tick of rubbing his neck when he responded to certain questions. The way he tried to divert the attention of being a cop away from himself and toward me. And, how he turned Dick onto a deal with Fat Willie and then Fat Willie paid with big bills.

I wanted to tell Dick that I thought his friend was a snitch, but I decided to wait.

I needed a little more time to think about it first.

To be sure.

# EIGHTEEN

# DICK

**MAKING** a conscious decision to be in a relationship isn't love, nor should it be confused as such. Being blindsided by heartfelt emotion and reacting based on those feelings, however, may be.

I made a conscious decision with Becky Baxter in ninth grade. It ended poorly. I believed I was in love, and Becky believed she wanted to make her previous boyfriend jealous. Being unaware of the previous boyfriend, and of her plan, I was shocked when the relationship abruptly ended, leaving me with a broken heart and nowhere to stick my over-anxious teenage dick.

The failed relationship nor the lesson in love ruined me from ever being in a meaningful relationship, but I always remembered it whenever I took the time to consider whether or not a relationship was a viable option.

With Jess, I had no time to consider. After close to a month, something just happened. The right time. The perfect person. I had no idea, all I knew was that I felt differently about her.

And it wasn't a decision I made.

"Love is *blank*. Finish that sentence."

"If I had to define it? Like make my own definition?" she asked.

"Yeah. Like shoot from the hip."

"I'm not good at this shit."

I twirled the spatula in my hand and admired her makeshift pajamas – my sweat pants and one of my white V-neck tee shirts. "Do your best."

"Love is when someone else's needs, wants, and desires come before your own," she said. "How's that?"

I shook the skillet and checked the consistency of the scrambled eggs. "Pretty good."

"Okay, now you."

Although I had asked the question, I wasn't as prepared as I thought I'd be. "Okay. Gimme a minute."

I stirred the eggs, decided they were done, and pulled the skillet from the stove. After I prepared the plates and we sat down, I took a bite and considered my response. Explaining how I felt, and how I had changed in the last month would be easier, but it wasn't necessarily what I was prepared to do.

I looked up from my plate. She was eating like she hadn't had a meal in days. I wondered if our previous night's sexual romp burned all of the calories she had in reserve. To go from living alone for my entire adult life to having her share a morning with me was a huge change, and watching her do simple things like eat or get dressed was rewarding.

I cleared my throat. "Love is when someone steps into your life, and instead of complicating it, they complete it."

She looked up from her plate. Her mouth was full of food. She didn't wait to swallow it before she commented. "Fat wuf fuckin awfumm."

I laughed. "What?"

She swallowed, took a drink of milk, and cleared her throat. "That was fucking awesome."

I took a make believe bow in recognition of her praise.

"Love is staying committed even when the other person loses devotion," she said.

I raised my eyebrows. "Excuse me?"

She shook her head. "Generic. That was generic. I wasn't throwing stones."

I poked a large chunk of scrambled eggs and lifted my fork to my mouth. "Love is recognizing all of the good in someone, seeing all the bad, and choosing to express the former and suppress the latter."

"Holy shit, Dude, I like that one," she said. Her eyes fell to her plate and she began to eat again. At about the time I wondered if we'd reached a point that we were done discussing the subject, she swallowed and fixed her eyes on mine. "Love is when your heart has feelings for a person that your mind is incapable of putting into words."

"And on that note, we should stop," I said. "That was good. I like that."

She smiled. "You know what?"

"What's that?"

"I used to be kind of scared that one day you'd just tell me to go away. And I hated the way I felt. When you were gone. And when you came back around I'd kind of forget the way I felt when you were gone. Now, when you're gone, I like it. I mean, I don't like it, but I do. Because I get all excited knowing that I'm going to see you again. The difference knowing and wondering is huge."

"And now you know?"

"Uh huh."

"How? How do you know I'm not going to decide to just leave you?"

"You don't trust people. You trust me." She shrugged.

"You're right."

She finished eating and shoved her plate to the side. "Want my opinion?"

I looked up from my plate. "Sure."

"Well, I've been thinking about a lot of stuff, and I made some notes. Hold on."

She jumped up, ran to my bedroom, and grabbed her purse. After pulling out her phone and scrolling through the screen, she looked up. "Ready?"

I found it cute that she asked me if I was *ready*. "I'm supposed to ask that."

She cocked an eyebrow.

"Yes," I said. "I'm ready."

She studied the screen on her phone. "Okay. Starting at the beginning. Drake said he just got the Corvette a few days before we got there, right?"

"That's what he said."

"Well, when we saw Beer Belly, he said he hadn't talked to Drake in a long time, but he asked you later if he let you drive the 'Vette. How would he know if Drake had a Corvette if he hadn't seen him or talked to him?"

I jumped from my seat. "Motherfucker. I didn't catch that."

My mind began spinning while thinking of the possibilities of Bart being arrested and turning snitch. Anything, I decided, was possible.

"There's a lot more," she said.

I began pacing the kitchen floor. "Keep going, I'm thinking."

She glanced at her phone. "Beer Belly set you up with Fat Willie, and Fat Willie paid you in new bills when he's always paid with his old

152

stash in the past. They were banded and all $100s. It might mean Beer Belly and Fat Willie are in cahoots with each other, and with the cops."

I stared at her in amazement. "How did you get all this on your phone?"

"I wrote a bunch of notes in my notepad last night after you fell asleep."

I nodded. "I like your way of thinking. Okay, keep going."

"Did Beer Belly himself tell you not to ever look at his scar, to look away?" she asked.

I chuckled. "He's made that clear. We all just make it a point to focus on something else, why?"

"I knew it!" she shouted. "He doesn't want you looking because he's got a tell-tale sign when he's nervous. He touches it. It's like a nervous tick. He did it when you asked if he'd heard from Drake, and when you asked about him setting you up with Fat Willie, when you asked about Drake, when he asked you if you wanted the diamond, and when I accused him of being a cop. Think about *that*."

"God damn, Jess. You think like a cop."

She grinned. "It's all the detective novels. And I've got more."

I sighed. "Let's hear it."

"The little Danny DeVito looking jeweler guy. You said when you went in with the diamond that he went to the back and made a call to investors. He's got a phone on the counter, why didn't he use it? I'll tell you why. Because he went to the back to make a call to have you smacked, that's why."

"Interesting," I said. "But what do we know from all of this? How is it going to help us with the diamond?"

She shrugged. "I don't know. But I say you need to stop trusting

Drake and Beer Belly both. And we just need to be prepared for the jeweler to try and steal the money, too."

"He's not going to steal the money," I said.

"How do you know?"

"Because you're going to have a little bit of real money, and a whole bunch of fake money."

She rubbed her hands together. "I like it."

"Now," I said. "You ready to plan the heist?"

She grinned from ear-to-ear. "*Heist*. I love it when you say things like that. It makes me wet."

I realized at that moment one thing that Jess and I shared. It was probably the biggest reason we got along so well. She loved mysteries, action, crime, and being involved in all facets of it. She said it excited her greatly just thinking about it. She'd spent her life reading books and daydreaming of the stories she read as if they were real.

When I planned a job, it often made my cock hard.

"You know," I said. "A true love for the game isn't something that can be taught, it's either part of who you are, or it isn't."

"By the game you mean the job? The heist?"

I nodded. "Yeah."

"You want the truth?" she asked.

"It's all I want," I responded.

"That's the first thing that attracted me to you. Threatening that guy in the alley. I love this shit."

At that moment, I was convinced.

Jess would never be a Becky Baxter.

# NINETEEN

## JESS

**DICK'S** discussion on the definition of love filled me with hope. I was convinced if I could be instrumental in helping him get the diamond back that he would accept me as being completely trustworthy, and our odd little relationship would flourish soon following.

"You ready?" he asked.

Chills went down my spine. "When you ask me that, my legs go weak."

"I'll take that as a *yes*."

He was dressed in sweats, a wife beater, and flip-flops. I really liked seeing him in a suit, and he looked great in slacks and a button-down, but nothing was better than seeing him wear a wife beater.

The muscles in his six-pack abs rippled through the material of the skin-tight shirt. His broad chest flared out the sides of the arm openings, and the tattoos on his right arm were visible. To me, the tattoos were confirmation of his bad boy status in the world, and seeing them made me wobbly-legged.

He began to pace the floor of his living room, talking as he walked. "Here's the plan. I'm assuming there's a cop in the mix somewhere. Actually, I'm banking on it. So, you'll meet the guy with the diamond at a public place. We'll try to get it at a supper club I know that's right off highway 35. It'll give us an easy exit. And you'll have your diamond expert with you. He'll inspect the stone, he'll test it to see if it's real, and you'll show them the money. They won't take time to count all the money in the bar, they'll either do it outside, or later. I guess all of that will depend on how much they trust you. My guess is $4,000,000 won't leave much room for trust, but cops always assume the money is real. They're less concerned with the money, because they want the arrest, not the cash. So, you check the diamond, give them the money, and at some point you're outside with the stone. And that's when the game changes."

I waved my hand in the air. "I have a question."

"Okay."

"How am I going to test a diamond to see if it's real?"

"Your accomplice will. He'll have an electronic diamond tester. It'll say if it's real or fake. They're 100% accurate."

I never heard of such shit. I found it fascinating. "Seriously?"

"Seriously."

"Okay, go ahead."

He started pacing again. "You get outside, and I'm going to be in the Ferrari waiting. Now, if there are cops, and I'm sure there will be, they'll let me sit there and wait without fucking with me, because they won't want to chance blowing their cover. So, even if they know it's me, they'll wait until the deal is done in hopes that they can arrest you and me in the car."

"Okay, so assume I've made it to the car with the diamond, then what?" I asked.

"This is the part you won't like," he said.

I laughed. I was ready to do whatever I had to do to get the diamond.

"As you say, I'm all ears."

"We're going to drive about a hundred feet, and while I'm rolling up to the intersection beside the bar, you'll open your door, and I'm going to toss your cute little ass out in the street. You'll roll into the middle of the intersection and start flailing around like you're hurt. Whoever is following me will stop, and that'll buy me just enough time to make sure I get out of there."

"Why the Ferrari? Won't they be looking for it after the chase?"

"It's the fastest car I've got, and they'll never fucking catch it, that's why."

"I fall out of the car and…"

"Pushed out. You get pushed out. It'll look like I used you to get the stone. They'll take you in, question you, and you'll tell them nothing of any substance. An attorney, who, ironically, will be your accomplice, will show up and get you out of the questioning. They'll never catch me, and I'll have the stone. I'll sell it in Houston for about $3,500,000, which will leave me about $2,000,000 up after the $500,000 I lose in the deal."

"Why will you lose $500,000?"

"It'll be the real money. The bait money."

"What will the rest be?"

"A damned good counterfeit."

I gasped. "You counterfeit money?"

"Hell no. But I bought some a long time ago. It'll pass for real, though."

"You bought counterfeit money? On purpose?"

"Bought $5,000,000 worth. It's good money for show. Paid $50,000 for it. I've used it over and over."

I sat and thought about all of the novels I had read over the years, and how the hero and the heroine always got away with similar heists. While lost in a daydream about one of the books, an idea came to me, causing me to chuckle a laugh. "I've got another idea that might just make this a foolproof plan and save you $500,000."

"I'm all ears."

"Well," I said. "It involves a fake 10 carat stone, and if I can get it to work, it just might save you your $500,000 in cash."

"Exchange stones?" he asked. "Deny the buy?"

"Something like that. Exchange stones, go to the bathroom. My accomplice walks out with the money. Everything would have to go perfect to do the switch, but it might work. I'll need a fake 10 carat stone and a pair of reading glasses."

He scrunched his nose. "Reading glasses?"

"Don't worry about it," I said. "I got this."

He nodded. "I like it. A lot."

I admired his physique and imagined us as an actual couple. Husband and wife, doing jobs and giving the money – part of it, at least – to people who really needed it. "I have more questions."

He grinned his shitty smirk. "I'm all ears."

"How am I going to carry $4,000,000."

"A million bucks in $100 bills only weighs 20 pounds. So four weighs 80 pounds. Two forty pound bags."

I assumed he knew what he was talking about, but it sure didn't seem right. "Twenty pounds? That doesn't seem like much."

"Believe me, that's what it weighs. It'll be like carrying a few bags of groceries. And, you'll have help."

"Okay, so what if there aren't any cops? What if we're scared for nothing?" I asked.

He shrugged. "It's that much better. We see who shows up. Maybe it's Danny DeVito, maybe someone else. Hell, maybe it's fucking Drake or Duc. But whoever it is will believe the money's real, and as long as the diamond's real, I've got my money back, and I'm up $2,000,000 or so.

"So we can't lose?"

"We can. We can get arrested for money laundering, possession of stolen property. Charged with burglarizing the football player's house. Possession of and use of counterfeit money in the furtherance of a crime. Hell, the list is long. State charges Federal charges. Probably talking about twenty years to life if we get caught. Which brings me to the last part."

"Which is?" I asked.

He stopped pacing. "Are you in, or are you out?"

I stood up, raised my hand in the air, and turned my palm to face him. "I'm in. All the way."

I was twenty-four years old. I had spent 16 of those years reading everything from Nancy Drew books to Robert Ludlum's books on Jason Bourne. I'd even read all of the Jack Reacher novels by Lee Child. My dream had always been to be involved in *something*. This was my one and only chance to do it.

He slapped his hand against mine. "That's my girl."

After hearing him say *that*, they could arrest me and toss me in prison. I wouldn't care. I was on top of the world.

# TWENTY

# DICK

**I** scanned the supper club for familiar faces and saw none. We'd just finished our last dance, and it was about time for me to depart. "You're meeting them in an hour, it's about time for me to go to the car."

We stood at the edge of the dancefloor. I was wearing a black tuxedo. Her hair was in a chignon with tendrils and she was dressed in a black dress, heels, and as much diamond jewelry as I could get her to wear. She defined elegance. Not the type of elegance than makes a man say *damn, she looks elegant*, but the type that sucks the breath from your lungs and causes you to stop dead in your tracks and take notice.

Together, we looked like we were on our honeymoon.

She locked eyes with me, gazed into my eyes for some time, and eventually sighed lightly. "I swear, if this deal works, this is the best day ever to replace my other best day ever."

"What happened on your other best day ever?"

She fanned her face with her hand and took a moment to catch her breath. "I got fucked before breakfast, after breakfast, and then got in a car chase with the cops. After that, I won $600 in a slot machine, and then got asked out on another date with the best criminal ever."

"Wow. And this will top that?"

She did her best to open her eyes wider than the slits she was looking

161

at me through. "Yeah. I love dancing, and we just danced for two hours. I feel like I'm going to barf, though."

"Maybe you shouldn't have had all that wine. And the margaritas."

She shrugged and offered a grin. "I'll be fine. Is this rain going to stop before this is over?"

"I don't know," I said. "I can't believe I left the umbrella in the car. It makes me sick to think about ruining your hair."

"I wasn't talking about my hair. A high speed getaway in the rain might be dangerous. Or impossible."

"Either way, I'll be faster than whoever's behind me."

She nodded. "True."

"Slow down on the drinking, maybe eat something. But I've got to get out of here. I don't want anyone to see me with you."

"Okay, just go, I'll be fine."

"You sure you're okay with everything?"

Her eyes thinned to slits. "I'm fine. We're in this together, Asshole. When are you going to believe me?"

"I believe you. And you've got that Glock in your purse. Don't forget that."

She waved her hand toward me, lost her balance, and about fell on the floor. "I know. Just go, before one of those snitches comes in here."

I reached for her face, steadied her jaw between my hands, and kissed her. The kiss was passionate, deep, and thought provoking. It made me want to stay, forget the diamond, and dance until we collapsed.

Our lips parted, and I released her. She stood, her mouth slightly agape, and stared blankly at me for a moment before it seemed that her eyes went into focus.

"Just go," she said. "If you stay for another minute we'll be arrested, and it won't be for theft. I'm gonna rape your sexy ass."

I glanced at my watch. I had fifty minutes. Reluctantly, I turned and walked away.

A quick scan of the dining area produced nothing out of the ordinary, and I recognized no one. I sauntered to the door, walked out into the rain, and inhaled a deep breath of the humid night air.

The supper club sat on a corner in a swanky district in Austin, with a main street that ran along the front of the building with valet parking, and a brick street at each side that was roughly two and a half lanes wide.

I planned on parking the Ferrari in along the brick street, hugging the side of the road, and waiting. I wouldn't look any different than any other asshole who drove a $300,000 Ferrari and parked in three parking spaces to keep his car from getting door dings.

I got the Ferrari from the parking garage and parked a block away. With the car running, and the windshield wipers dancing back and forth, I watched the entrance like a hawk.

My buzzing phone startled me.

A number I didn't recognize.

I answered. "This is Dick."

*"Mr. Wiltshire?"*

"Yes."

*"This is Supervisory Officer Willis with TSA. We have a leopard you're going to need to pick up."*

*Oh shit.*

"It's really a bad time for me. Can I get it tomorrow?"

*"That is a negative,"* he said. *"The cat will be required to be picked up before 10:00 pm. Several messages have been left unanswered."*

*Fuck.*

"Can someone sign for it besides me?"

*"As long as they have I.D."*

"I'll have someone pick it up."

*"The animal will be at the United baggage check. You should be able to park in the unloading lane and come in through the turnstile."*

"I'll get it taken care of."

*"Thank you, Sir, and have a nice night."*

I hung up. The last thing I needed was to have a fucking leopard in the car.

I scrolled through my contacts, stopped at *Seton*, and pressed the call button.

*"Hello? Everything a go?"*

"I need you to stop really quick on your way."

*"Really quick? I'm on my way now."*

"It'll be ten minutes out of your way. Stop at the airport, park at the terminal's unloading lane for United, and go to baggage check. There's a leopard in my name.

*"A leopard?"*

"Yeah, a cat."

*"You're having me pick up a leopard? Now?"*

"God damn it, Seton. I'm not going to fucking argue with you. Get the cat and hurry the fuck up. Don't make me..." I pulled the phone from my ear and glared at it. "Just get the fucking cat."

Frustrated about it all, I hung up.

Aggravated, I surveyed the street, the supper club, and the surrounding area. At 9:25, what I was sure was an unmarked police car parked half a block behind me. Two idiots sat in the car smoking cigarettes and talking.

Typical cops doing a half-assed surveillance job.

I checked my pistol, assured myself it was loaded and ready, and shifted my eyes from the rearview mirror to the door of the club.

It was eerie how natural it felt having Jess involved with the job. I trusted her wholly and completely, which was something had never done. My life of crime had been performed single-handedly, and I had every expectation of continuing my modus operandi for as long as I was in the business.

Now, however, I couldn't imagine doing anything without Jess' help. Her love of criminal suspense novels caused her to develop a keen eye and a criminal mind.

My only concern was being one hundred percent certain that she wasn't harmed.

If anyone damaged as much as a hair on her head, I wouldn't be in prison for counterfeit money, laundering cash, or stealing a diamond.

I'd be locked away for murder.

# TWENTY-ONE

## JESS

**I** sat at the table with Seton, who, ironically, was the man Dick was threatening the day I met him in the alley. With the money between us on the floor and a briefcase on the table, we sat and talked about everything under the sun while we waited.

"You're clear on if I go to the bathroom, you need to wait just a minute, secure the money, and then act concerned, right?"

"That's exactly what I'll do. He'll have the fake stone. No one in their right mind would leave the cash and the stone at the table. I'll pick up the money and say I'm checking on you."

Out of my peripheral I saw someone who caught my attention. It was rather strange, because he was a hundred feet from me, but his manner of walking gave me pause.

I shifted my eyes from Seton toward the man, and realized it was the man with the mustache from the soup kitchen.

"Holy shit," I whispered, "That man over there by the bathrooms is the mustache man."

Seton didn't turn his head, but he shifted his eyes toward the bathrooms. "Blue shirt, blue slacks?"

"Yeah."

I tried to shake off my drunkenness, but it wasn't possible. I squinted and tried to look like I was focused elsewhere while I watched him. "He's the one who was talking to Drake and Duc at the soup kitchen."

"He's a cop."

My eyes shot to Seton. "Is that an opinion or fact?"

"Fact."

"How do you know?"

"I've seen him in court. He's a detective."

"I fucking knew it," I whispered. "Which means Duc and Drake are either snitches or they're being investigated."

He turned his head to the side, gazed off in the distance for a moment, and then agreed. "I'd say you're right. They're probably both."

I didn't like Drake from the minute that hotdog eating motherfucker tried to shake my hand. And Duc looked scary, and not the sexy kind of scary, the scary kind of scary.

Seton sighed lightly. "Let's hope he's not the guy who's meeting us. He may recognize me. It's been a few years, but I'm sure it's him. Detective Ortiz."

"What if you introduce yourself as my legal counsel?" I asked. "You could be my legal consultant and my diamond expert. It might make us look more valid. More, I don't know, real."

"Not a bad idea," he said.

Mustache man started walking in our direction. When it was apparent he was going to be the one who met us, I stood up.

"Hi, I'm Mrs. Wheeler."

"Thurston Tribideaux," he said, "The third. I'm a broker with Southern Equity."

"Seton Hallsworth," Seton said. "I'll be acting as Mrs. Wheeler's legal counsel throughout the transaction."

Tribideaux didn't flinch. "Very well." He glanced around, must have accepted the dining areas as safe, and reached into his jacket pocket.

He reached toward Seton and handed him a folded cloth. "The stone."

*Fuck yes. This might work.*

While Seton unfolded the cloth, I leaned onto the top of the table and turned up my southern Texas accent. A whiff of an unidentifiable something caused my nostrils to flare. I shook it off and smiled at the mustache man. "I must apologize in advance, Mr. Tribideaux. I've been so darned excited for the last few hours, I'm as drunk as a skunk, as loose as a goose, and my pea sized bladder is as full as a tick on a bloodhound's ear."

"Apology accepted," he said with a laugh. "And my condolences regarding the loss of your husband."

"Preston was a fine man for sure. He'll be so pleased about this." I reached over and placed my hand on top of his. "As long as this diamond checks out."

His caterpillar lip almost made me barf. He chuckled a deep but very brief laugh. "I'm sure you'll find it to your satisfaction."

Seton looked puzzled. He poked the diamond, stared down at his tester, poked it again, and sighed heavily. "The tester appears to be malfunctioning. I can't get an accurate reading. It's telling me the stone is a fake. Let's proceed under the belief that everything checks out."

*What the fuck?*

*Diamond specialist my ass.*

*Proceed under the belief?*

"How sad," I said, trying to hide the fact I was about to barf.

Seton turned toward me. "Would you like to see it?"

I nodded. I felt sick at my stomach. I coughed a light laugh and extended my open palm. "Is a pig's ass made of pork?"

Seton handed me the cloth with the diamond folded into it. As I accepted it, he winked at me with his eye that was out of Tribideaux's view.

It was all I had to go on, but I assumed everything was a go.

I found out through the education I received from Dick that a 10 carat diamond is barely over one half of an inch in diameter. In comparison, a dime was 50% larger in diameter than a 10 carat stone.

Making it very, very easy to conceal.

I unfolded the cloth, looked at the stone, and squinted. "I can't see a darned thing without my glasses," I said. "Forgive me."

I held the cloth above the table in my left hand so not to raise suspicion. With my right hand, I reached below the table and into my purse. After retrieving the fake stone and my glasses, I cupped the stone in my palm and lifted the glasses to my face.

I rested the glasses against the bridge of my nose. "Let me have a look."

I unfolded the cloth and pinched the stone between the thumb and forefinger of my right hand. Now holding both stones in my right hand, one in my palm, and one in my fingers, I stared down at it and let out a laugh.

"It's seems so small without being set into a ring. Seton, dear, do you have one of those little thingies?"

He chuckled. "A loop?"

"Whatever you call it." I chuckled.

He reached into his jacket pocket and produced a loop. As I reached for it, I loosened my grip, dropped the fake stone into the cloth, and rolled the real stone into my palm.

*So far, so good.*

I lifted the loop to my glasses, chuckled, and set the loop on the edge of the table. "I guess I don't need these glasses after all."

While holding the cloth and diamond well above the table, I leaned over and dropped my glasses and the real stone in my purse.

"Let me have a look," I said.

Seton studied the mustache man, and I studied the diamond. It seemed, for the time being, that everyone was happy. I looked at the stone for a few long seconds. It was pretty, but indiscernible from the fake. It was roughly the size of a Cheerio and worth almost $4,000,000, which I found to be ridiculous.

"Oh my, that is a pretty one, isn't it?" I asked, although it wasn't anything special.

My nostrils flared again. I handed Seton the loop and fanned my face with my free hand. "Reminds me of when Preston proposed to me."

Seton lowered his head. "God rest his soul."

*Nice addition.*

I gave Seton the open cloth with the diamond in full view. "Mr. Tribideaux, forgive me. I must retire to the powder room for a moment."

The mustache stood up. Seton stood up. I stood, grabbed my purse, and did my best to keep from running. So far, everything had gone as planned and I was as happy as a little drunken thief could be.

In my walk to the bathroom, I realized I was slightly drunker than I remembered being when I sat down. It happened to me quite frequently. From the time I stopped drinking until the time I was the drunkest seemed to be roughly two hours apart.

Once in the bathroom, I was so excited that I almost couldn't pee.

After a long wait, I finally did, and only after I was finished did I text Dick.

I opened the bathroom door slightly, made sure the coast was clear, and nonchalantly began walking toward the front door. Seton faced me, and Tribideaux had his back to me. As long as Tribideaux didn't turn around, I knew I could make it.

I heard the unmistakable rumble of the Ferrari's exhaust. I glanced at Seton. He nodded. Kind of. Not a conventional nod, but an unmistakable lowering of the chin. An undercover clandestine nod.

It was my cue.

I ducked behind a couple who was walking in, pushed the front door open, and peered through it. The rain had stopped, but the streets were still wet. The many colors of the neon signs from the adjoining bars reflected off of the asphalt, making the scene seem slightly romantic.

I glanced to the right. Sitting in the Ferrari fifteen feet from the door, he sat in wait.

*Dick.*

The beauty of our escape, the $3,500,000 diamond, the red Ferrari, outsmarting the mustache cop, it was just too much. My pussy was soaked. I was suffering from an alcohol induced sensory overload.

I glanced left. A car was on the same side of the street as Dick, thirty feet behind him. The headlights were off, but exhaust bellowed from the rear of the car.

The outline of two men was unmistakable.

And one had a mustache. Undoubtedly a cop.

I ran to the Ferrari, pulled open the door, and jumped inside. "I've got it!" I shouted.

"Atta girl!" Dick hollered.

I tossed my purse on the floor. "Seton's gonna get the cash. Go!"

Dick hit the throttle, causing the car to spin out on the wet pavement. Flashing lights reflecting off of the wet street caught my attention. I spun around. The car behind us had an undercover cop light on the dash.

"There's a cop behind us!" I shouted.

"Fucker's been there all night," he said.

Still peering through the back window, my eyes fell to the narrow flat space behind the seats of the car. A cage filled the space. Inside, a small leopard paced back and forth, growling.

I blinked a few times. I was drunk, but I wasn't *that* drunk. "Dick there's a spotted cat in the back."

"Yeah, it was kind of gonna be a surprise."

The cat stopped pacing and locked eyes with me. It was creepy. And beautiful. Reluctantly, I broke its stare.

Dick hit the gas again, and the car spun out.

"Motherfucking rain," he snarled.

Each time the car spun out, the traction control kicked in. This would cause the car's tires to stop spinning, and limit the engine's power. Dick fumbled with the dash, found the button to disable it, and glanced toward me.

"Ready?"

*Music to my ears.*

"Fuck yes," I said.

"It's gonna get hairy."

As far as I was concerned, 700 horsepower in the rain with no traction control wasn't *hairy*, it was exciting. I grinned and nodded my drunken head. "Just go!"

I no more than spoke, and Dick's door flew open. Startled, I screamed. Dick tried to drive away, but someone grabbed him by the jacket and yanked him halfway out of the car.

Scared, confused, and not ready for anything of the sort, my eyes frantically darted around the interior of the car for anything I could grab to help. The dull *thud* of fists hitting flesh was more prominent than anything else. I felt sick.

*The umbrella.*

I grabbed the umbrella and waved it across the interior of the car toward Dick's right hand – the only portion of him still in the car.

"Dick, here!" I yelled.

The umbrella tapped against his hand a few times. Finally, he gripped it firm.

I glanced toward the cop car. The passenger door opened. The cop with the mustache got out. The sound of an agonizing groan caused me to shift my focus toward Dick. He threw one last punch, knocking the man into the street.

He jumped in the car, got situated, and tossed the umbrella in my lap.

My head spun to the rear. Mustache got back in the cop car. The leopard growled. Everything was happening so fast that it seemed my mind's attempt to process it was making me sick. I grabbed the umbrella and tossed it aside.

The unmistakable smell of blood filled the car. I glanced down at my hand. "I'm bleeding!"

"It's the umbrella," Dick said. "I stabbed that guy with it."

Without warning, Dick hit the gas. The car shot forward, spinning the tires the entire time. The engine revved, the sound of the exhaust screamed out the back, and in an instant we were on our way to an easy escape.

At the upcoming intersection, two horses began to slowly walk past in front of us. The district we were in had carriage rides through downtown, and, as fate would have it, one was directly in front of us.

"Horse!" I shouted.

Dick screamed and hit the brakes. I glanced to the rear. The cops were only a few feet behind us. Mustache got out.

The sound of gunfire rang out, and the back window of the car shattered.

"Those motherfuckers," Dick shouted as he swerved the car to the left, almost into the oncoming lane.

"What are you doing?" I shouted.

"Open your door. Time for you to get out."

I didn't want to. I wanted to stay with him. I wanted to escape. The plan came together and we were one horse drawn carriage ride away from escaping the perfect crime.

The sound of another gunshot shot made me flinch.

Dick pulled out his gun. "If those motherfuckers hit you or my cat…"

The carriage was almost past.

"Open your door!" he demanded.

Reluctantly, I did as he asked.

"Ready?" he asked.

I wasn't.

I inhaled a deep breath and nodded.

And he pushed me out of the car and into the wet street.

# TWENTY-TWO

# DICK

**JESS** fell out of the car with the finesse of a trained Hollywood stuntwoman. When she hit the ground, she rolled into the center of the street and stretched out like she'd been killed.

The cops who were following me slammed on the brakes. Physically unable to drive around her, and bound by sworn oath to provide her assistance, it appeared they were doing just that. I turned to the right, hit the gas, and intentionally spun the car into a 180 degree turn, shooting off to the left. The car slid sideways, and the engine revved as I fishtailed up the street toward the highway.

A quick check of the rearview mirror produced no one. Nonetheless, I hammered the gas, sped toward the highway on-ramp, and hoped there were no more cops on my tail.

Once on the highway, the roads had been traveled enough that they were dry from the early evening Texas rainstorm. I didn't need to be in a chase with the police if I didn't have to be, and as it appeared, I was alone in my travels.

I slowed to 70 miles an hour, checked my mirrors periodically, and couldn't help but laugh when I pulled off the highway fifteen minutes later with not a soul in sight.

Feeling rather anxious, I pulled over in a hardware store parking

177

lot and set the parking brake. I grabbed Jess' purse, scanned through contents, and found nothing.

I looked again.

*Nothing.*

One item at a time, I removed each and every article from her purse.

*Nothing.*

Frustrated, I tossed the purse beside the growling leopard, and scanned the passenger side floor.

A glistening from the center of the floor mat shot a glimmer of hope through my bloodstream. I got out of the car, walked to the passenger door, and opened it. I stared down at the floorboard where Jess' purse had been, and immediately grinned.

Against the black carpeting, the 10 carat stone looked like a fascinating pebble.

A $3,500,000 pebble.

I picked it up, held it under the streetlight, and smiled at the thought of it all.

My life was almost in order.

All I needed was one more thing.

Jess.

# TWENTY-THREE

# JESS

**I** wasn't hurt at all, but tried to act like I was half-dead. Two men from the carriage hopped out and ran toward me.

"Don't fucking move," one of the cops yelled.

I wasn't going anywhere. I was too drunk, and kind of sore. "I'm not," I murmured.

"I said don't fucking move," he yelled again.

Apparently, he was talking to the fifty-year-old dude with the red hair who was walking over to see if I was hurt.

"I'll shoot your dumb ass where you stand, Motherfucker."

I looked toward the cop.

*Oh. My. God.*

His lip was covered in an award-winning porno 'stache. I almost barfed.

I glanced toward the two men from the carriage.

"Lower your fahkin' weapon," the red-haired man said. "Ian Earling, I'm an ambassador..."

"Keep your hands where I can see them." The cop interrupted.

"Fahk off," his partner shouted. "I'll have yahr fahkin' job."

"Ambassador?" the cop asked. "Did you say you're an ambassador?"

"You're fahking right. Republic of Ireland."

"You have papers?"

"You'll see 'em when I see yer badge."

I glanced at the mustache toting cop. Another cop was standing to the side, hiding behind the cover of the car with his gun drawn as well.

*Holy shit.*

Badges and diplomatic immunity paperwork were exchanged. Apologies were given, and weren't necessarily accepted. I wondered if I could leave. No one seemed to be paying attention to me. I pressed my palms into the wet street, raised myself from the ground, and attempted to stand.

The cop at the car yelled for me to get on the ground.

"You, in the dress, don't fucking move!"

*Jesus.*

My knees ached. Other than that I was a little wet, but unharmed. I stood as still as I could.

"Get on the ground."

"I just got up."

"Get on the fucking ground," he barked.

I pressed my hands to my hips. "Are you fucking kidding me?"

"I've got her, Joe," mustache said. He placed his hand against my shoulder. "Come with me, Lady."

"Am I under arrest?"

He tugged me toward the car. "I said come with me."

I shot him a shitty drunken glare. "I asked you a question."

"You're being detained. Get in the car."

*Detained.*

*Sounds official.*

He pushed me against the car. "I'm going to pat you down, it's

180

policy."

"Enjoy yourself," I said in a sarcastic tone.

He frisked me. "No I.D. No purse, no anything?"

"I travel light."

"What were you doing in the club?"

I saw no reason to lie, and from what Dick said, if everything went our way – which it did – I could tell them the truth.

I turned around. The top of his mustache crept into his mouth. My stomach convulsed. "I was buying a diamond."

He pulled against it with his bottom lip. "Were you, now?"

I looked away. "I was trying."

He cleared his throat. "Why'd you come outside?"

I focused on cop number two. He looked like a game show host. "I was planning on barfing."

"What stopped you?"

I turned to face mustache. "From?"

"Barfing?"

"I saw the guy in the Ferrari. I thought he left earlier. You know, when he left. When I saw him, I just got in his car. He told me to get out, and I told him I wanted to suck him off. I tried to suck his cock, and he tossed me out in front of the horses."

"Looked like you had a purse when you got in the car. Where's your purse?"

I looked away. I'd reached my mustache quota for the month. "I'm drunk as fuck. I don't know where my ass is right now, let alone my purse."

He laughed. "So you were buying a diamond, decided to barf, and hopped in a car to suck a guy off. Was he paying you for that blowjob?"

"I'm not a whore, Asshole."

"Givin' 'em away, huh?"

"He was a good dancer." I shrugged. "I thought maybe…"

"Where's the diamond?"

I tossed my head toward the supper club. "Last I saw it; it was down there."

"Load her up," cop two barked.

Mustache tugged against my shoulder. "We're taking you in for questioning."

"Can we stop for a cheeseburger?"

He shot me an evil glare with a mustache accoutrement. "You got a lot of nerve."

"I've got a full bladder, sore knees, and I'm fucking hungry."

"No, we're not stopping for a cheeseburger. Give us some information about your partner, and we'll see if we can get you a cup of coffee."

"My partner?"

"Yeah."

"Her name's Katie. She likes threesomes and being fisted. Probably right up your alley. You're in the industry, right?"

He did look like a porn star. I thought he might appreciate the remark.

I was wrong.

"You smart-mouthed little bitch."

Dick could call me a bitch. I found it on the cusp of being cute. Anyone else? Yeah, not so much.

"Fuck off, pig."

The game show host loosened his tie and opened the door. Mustache pushed me into the back seat.

"What time is it?" I asked.

"10:00 straight up," Mustache answered.

They could do whatever they wanted.

But if everything went as planned, it'd only last an hour.

# TWENTY-FOUR

# DICK

**NOT** knowing Jess' status weighed down on me hard. I sat in the kitchen sipping whiskey feeling that the recovery of the diamond – and my investment money – wasn't as important as I had previously believed.

Had she been gone shopping or at work, an hour would have passed in what seemed like a matter of seconds. Having no idea if she was safe, however, seemed to make time stand still. I began to regret the heist. Forfeiting Jess and gaining the diamond wasn't a trade I was now willing to do.

But the deal was done.

I found out through the course of everything that trading Jess for $3,500,000 wasn't a trade I was willing to do.

Jess was priceless.

I grew up in a very wealthy home, the child of a father who made his money off of other people's investments. When the recession of 2008 hit, people under my father's financial watch lost everything, while he continued to get even richer. Many lost their jobs, homes, and other material possessions. Yet others lost their ability to see a bright enough future to continue, and committed suicide.

Respect was something my father never earned from me. As a child, being alone because none of the other children were financially worthy of being my friend made some sense at first, but as I grew older, it made no sense. I grew to despise my father's prosperity, his belief that the gap between the rich and the poor was never great enough, and his manner of feeding his growing wealth.

I sat at the bar drinking my whiskey and staring at the diamond wondering if I was slowly becoming more like him. The proceeds from the diamond were never going to be used for personal reasons, only for causes I believed to be worthy of receiving the wealth. Nonetheless, Jess' absence made me feel I had paid the ultimate price for the stone.

My phone buzzed.

I jumped from my seat and ran to the end of the bar.

Seton.

"What the fuck?" I asked as I answered.

"Five minutes out."

Damn, that was quick.

"Everything good?"

"Everything's great."

I had Jess' purse, cell phone, and all of her personal items, so I realized she couldn't call me. But. I just wanted to hear her voice.

"Let me talk to Jess."

"I don't have Jess."

"You *what*?"

"I'll see you in a minute, I'm 60 seconds away."

"Where is she."

"I'll see you in a second."

"Where the fuck is she?"

"Police station."

"God damn you, Seton. I'll slaughter your entire family if something happens to her. I swear."

"Pulling in now."

The phone went dead.

*Fuck!*

"What the fuck's going on?" I screamed as he walked through the front door.

He stopped at the threshold. "Quit being a prick and go get the money. I've got to swap some things around. I need a small screwdriver set."

"Where's Jess?"

"I told you. The police station. I need to do a few things before I go get her."

I walked around the corner of the bar and began to stomp my way to where he was standing. "Like fucking what?" I snarled.

"Like making sure they can't charge her with a crime. Grab that money and get me that screwdriver set."

"You've got the money?"

He nodded. "All of it."

Having the money was reassuring, but I wanted the girl. I stomped out to the car, grabbed the money, and stomped back into the house.

I tossed the money on the entry hall floor and turned toward the garage. After digging through my toolbox, I returned with a small set of jeweler's tools.

"Here."

He carried his diamond tester to the bar, disassembled it, and began to pry against the circuit board with one of the screwdrivers.

"What the fuck are you doing?"

He lowered the tool, sighed, and turned to face me. "I tested the stone. It was authentic. I said it didn't test out. Your plan, Dick, had a hole in it. Now, what I need to do is disable this tester to make it inoperative, go to the police station, and in the event that the question arises – and I suspect it may – I can back up my end of the story. They have a fake 10 carat diamond, but they *may* have a real one that I am unaware of. This way I'm covered no matter what."

"You lost me."

"I'm not surprised," he said.

"Don't start getting smart with me, you motherfucker. I'll…"

"Give it a rest, Dick." He screwed the back onto the tester, slid it into his leather satchel, and glared at me for a second.

"See you in an hour," he said as he turned away.

I had no idea what his ridiculous plan was fucking up his tester, but he was the attorney, and I wanted to assume he knew what the fuck he was doing.

He paused as he reached for the door. "Where's the crazy cat?"

*Oh fuck.*

# TWENTY-FIVE

# JESS

*10:40 p.m. the day of the heist*

**I** stepped out of the bathroom and into the hallway. I didn't want to go back into the interrogation room, I wanted to buy some more time.

"You do realize it'll be in your best interest to tell us everything you know, right?" Necktie asked.

I shot him a confused look. "I don't *know* shit. I'm fucking drunk."

"I know some things," he said with sarcastic tone. "I know you're in a hell of a mess."

"I danced with some hot guy. I tried to buy a diamond. I got up to pee, and my fucking head started spinning. I peed and thought I was good to go, and halfway back to my seat, I got a case of bubble guts. I went outside for fresh air. No crimes committed, *Officer.*"

"There's more to it than that. Your story might change when we get back in the interrogation room."

"What about that coffee?" I asked.

My tongue felt dry and calloused. I repeatedly pressed it to the roof of my mouth to try and clean it off, but each time I felt like I was going to puke as a result. Coffee wouldn't cure me, but it damned sure couldn't hurt.

"What time is it?" I asked.

"10:40."

He got me my coffee, and I followed him back to the interrogation room. He pushed the door open, and upon entering the room, I got two nice little surprises.

One, Tribideaux was waiting.

And two, I identified the smell that caused my nostrils to flare in the supper club.

*Cinnamon.*

I acted uninterested in Tribideaux's presence. "It smells like fucking Christmas in here," I said.

"Sit down," Porn 'stache demanded.

I tried to steady my cup of coffee. "I'm working on it."

I sat down and glanced at each of the three men. I had no idea where they were going to go with the conversation, so I decided to start my own.

I shot Tribideaux a sultry grin. "Did you bring the diamond?"

"Shut up, I'm asking the questions. Mrs. Preston Wheeler, my ass. Where's your I.D.?" Tribideaux snapped.

I took a sip of my coffee and tried not to smile. "I have no idea."

"Where's the diamond?" he asked.

There were two too many mustaches in the room. I turned to the side and tried to focus on the necktie-wearing cop. "I gave it to my attorney when I went to the bathroom."

Necktie slapped his hand against the edge of the table. "What did you do with the diamond?"

I wasn't scared of their good cop – bad cop routine. I met his gaze with my best drunken laser sharp glare. "Weren't you listening?"

His eyes narrowed to slits. "Lying to an officer in the course of an investigation. Five years. Theft of a $4,000,000 diamond. Ten years. Obstruction of justice. Twenty-four months. Want me to continue?"

I took a sip of coffee and wondered where Seton was. I didn't like hearing how many years they were going to lock me up for. Even if it was bullshit.

I held his gaze for as long as I could. "No."

He straightened his posture and nodded his head toward Tribideaux. "Let me introduce Federal Agent Whitmire. You might know him as Tribideaux. Your world is preparing to collapse, little girl. Do you know what they do to girls like you in prison?"

My mouth went dry. I turned toward Tribideaux-Whitmire and tried to swallow, but got nothing but dust.

I took a sip of coffee and tried to force a smile. My face contorted into a drunken smirk.

Tribideaux-Whitmire crossed his arms in front of his chest. "You are in the middle of a joint investigation between the FBI, the state of Texas, and US Marshall Service regarding large-scale thefts and the money that is being laundered as a result of said thefts. Life. To the bitter end. That is what we're talking about, not ten or fifteen measly years. Your cute little ass will rot in prison. Now I'm going to ask questions, and you're going to provide answers, understand?"

I nodded.

"18 USC, section 1001. Lying to a Federal Officer in the course of an investigation. It'll get you 120 months. That's ten years, not five. All you have to do is tell me one little lie. Just one. No matter what else happens here tonight, if you lie once to *me*, you'll go away for a dime piece."

191

He leaned over the table and got so close I could feel his breath. "You look pale, little girl. Are you scared?"

I was. But I trusted Dick. I shook my head in support of my claim. "No."

"You should be."

I took a sip of coffee. "I'm scared of mustaches."

The look on his face confirmed he didn't appreciate my sense of humor. "Who's the guy in the Ferrari?"

I shrugged. "Some guy I was wanting to fuck."

*That wasn't a lie at all.*

He shook his head in disgust. "What is his name?"

I glanced at the clock. 10:50. I needed to buy some time. Ten minutes if Seton was on time.

"His name?"

"Yes, god damn it, his name."

"Dick."

So far, I was on a roll for telling the truth.

He reached up and twisted his mustache between his thumb and index finger. I glanced at Necktie. His mouth was curled into a perma-grin. My eyes drifted to Porn 'stache. He was scratching his nuts and staring at the dirt under his fingernails.

Tribideaux-Whitmire broke the awkward silence. "When you snuck outside, you had your purse. Where's your purse now?"

"I don't know."

I did a mental fist pump. Hell, it was easy not lying.

"Did you leave it in the car?"

I cleared my throat. "I didn't leave it anywhere. I was pushed out into the street and was almost trampled to death by two fucking

Clydesdales."

Also true. The death by slow-moving Clydesdales was a matter of opinion, but I doubted he could prove beyond a shadow of doubt to a court of law that I wasn't in danger.

I chocked it up as another truthful response.

The door swung open. "Legal counsel for the lady," an officer said.

I turned toward the voice.

*Seton.*

*Thank God.*

Seton reached into his pocket, removed a small gold case, and tossed three business cards on the table. It was time for shit to get real, and I was ready.

He brushed the lapels of his suit coat. "Gentlemen, Seton Allen Hallsworth, Esquire. The questioning will now be directed to me, and my client will only respond to questions I advise her to be in her best legal interest."

"You phony turd," Tribideaux-Whitmire said. "One of you two fuck-nuggets switched out the diamond on me."

"An accusation such as that will not be taken lightly, Sir. Your diamond didn't check out as being authentic. That, Sir, cannot be refuted. For the safety of my client, and in anticipation of being swindled, I recorded the entire conversation," Seton said.

He reached into his jacket, removed a small device, and pressed his thumb against it.

*"As long as this diamond checks out."*

*"I'm sure you'll find it to your satisfaction."*

*"The tester appears to be malfunctioning. I can't get an accurate reading. It's telling me the stone is a fake. Let's proceed under the belief*

*that everything checks out."*

*"How sad."*

*"Would you like to see it?"*

*"Is a pig's ass made of pork?"*

He pressed his thumb against it again, stopping it. He grinned and placed the recorder in his inner jacket pocket.

Tribideaux-Whitmire looked angry. "The diamond was authentic."

"Federal Rule of Evidence Rule 901," Seton said in a matter-of-fact tone. "Otherwise known as the Authentication of Identification Rule, requires that the chain of custody for evidence be maintained. I'll ask, Good Sir, if you could provide the chronological support to me for review."

I had no idea what he was saying, but I really liked what everyone's faces did.

*Hashtag sad face.*

A hand hit the table. "That fucking diamond was authentic."

I looked up. Agent Tribideaux-Whitmire looked as though he swallowed a spoonful of something bitter.

"According to my tester, Sir, it was not. My tester wasn't checked prior to our meeting, and could certainly be out of calibration, but there is no law in place to require me to test it or to calibrate it. There is, however such law in place to require you, Sir, to prove you had the diamond tested prior to the meeting. If you are unable to prove its authenticity was verified prior to the meeting, as a matter of law you may not claim its inauthenticity following the meeting."

*Silence.*

"Based on your allegations, I would have assumed the diamond *was* tested prior to the meeting," Seton said. "However, your three somber faces tell me otherwise."

Tribideaux-Whitmire cleared his throat. "I think your tester works just fine, and you're full of shit, Counselor."

Seton coughed a light laugh. "My tester is not the subject of this discussion; your chain of evidence is. For the sake of entertainment, have you the stone?"

Tribideaux-Whitmire looked sick. He reached into his jacket pocket. The cloth and stone were produced.

Seton reached into his pocket, removed the tester, and poked the diamond with a small prod. A red light illuminated. He turned the tester toward each of the officers. They acted uninterested.

Porn 'stache scratched his nuts.

"I will ask one last time." Seton sighed and placed the tester in his pocket. "Did you check your stone for authenticity immediately prior to the meeting, and if your response is *yes*, I need to see the document supporting said test as well as the credentials of the person who performed the test.

"Fuck you, Counselor," Tribideaux-Whitmire said.

"As I suspected." Seton reached for my hand. "We'll be leaving now."

"This isn't over," Porn 'stache warned.

"As a matter of law," Seton said. "It is over. Any questions for this client will henceforth be directed to me. Without the authentication for the diamond, the only crime committed is detaining my client. Any attempts to question her will be considered harassment, and will be met with a civil action lawsuit against the state and the federal government."

I stood up, reached for my coffee, and drank it in one gulp. "Gentlemen."

# DICK

Seton motioned toward the door. "After you."

And, just like that, all my worries washed away.

# TWENTY-SIX

# DICK

**"OH** my God," Jess gasped as soon as she walked into the house. "What happened?"

My face, neck, shoulders, and arms were covered in blood. "I was attacked," I said.

"Jesus fucking Christ," Seton breathed. "You look like death."

"Believe me," I said. "Whatever it looks like, it feels worse."

"Knife fight?" Jess asked as she got closer.

Embarrassed, I shook my head. "The leopard."

Jess laughed. "The spotted cat? It attacked you?"

I nodded. "It's evil. If I can find it, it's going up for auction."

"The fucker growled the entire time it was in my car, I can say that much," Seton said.

I turned toward Jess and opened my arms. "So, it sounds like everything went good. No surprises?"

Seton shook his head. "Just as I suspected, they couldn't prove that they maintained a chain of evidence. Without proof that they tested the diamond immediately prior to the meeting, they couldn't accuse us of switching it. Ninety percent of the time they can't prove a maintained chain of evidence."

"Interesting."

Jess hugged me. I wanted to kiss her, but my face felt like it was afire. Covered with small – and large – lacerations, I looked like I had been in a knife fight with a hundred Ninja masters.

"You look awful," she said.

"Forget me. Your performance in this thing was top fucking notch," I said. "When you rolled out of the car, I almost died laughing. Out there in the middle of the street with your arms and legs stretched out…"

"I was trying to take up the entire street. I wanted to make sure they couldn't get past me." She chuckled. "And they didn't."

"And what about those fucking horses." I chuckled. "When you screamed 'horse!' I about shit."

"Horse!" she screeched.

The three of us shared a laugh.

I caught my breath and looked at Seton. "Did we learn how the fuck they got the diamond? Who attacked me at the jewelers?"

He shrugged. "Haven't yet."

Jess' eyes shot wide and she gasped. "I almost forgot. The man with the mustache from the soup kitchen was the man at the supper club. He's a Federal Agent. Whitmire. Anyway, guess fucking what?"

"What?"

"Well," she said. "When we were at the supper club, I kept smelling something and it was about to make me sick. Every time I leaned over to talk to mustache man, it would make my nose burn. I didn't get it at first, but when I walked into the interrogation room after I peed, I smelled it again. Guess what the mustache man smelled like?"

I shrugged. "What?"

"Cinnamon!"

I shrugged again. "And…"

"Beer Belly. The cinnamon house."

I nodded. "Interesting. We'll need to look into that. I'm guessing someone got to him, though. Turned him into a snitch."

"Agreed," Seton said.

"So where's the cat?"

"I have no idea. I opened the cage, and it jumped out and just sat down. It looked like it was breathing pretty heavy, and I figured it was scared so I reached down to pick it up. As soon as I touched it, it started swinging its paws at me. Next thing I knew, I was covered in blood and it was gone."

Jess laughed. "I'm sorry. It's just. It's a *cat*. I can't believe it did that to you."

I felt I needed to correct her. It wasn't a cat. Not even close. "It's a thirty-pound *leopard*. They said it'll get up to fifty pounds."

She studied my cuts and shook her head. "And you haven't seen it since?"

I shook my head. "Not once."

"Did you put some food out for it?"

"That's another thing. All it can eat is raw chicken."

"What? Raw meat?"

"Chicken. That's it. I bought some the other day, it's in the fridge."

She laughed. "I'll put some out. I'm guessing you found the diamond?"

"On the floorboard of the car. I was scared for a minute when I didn't find it in your purse."

"I'm so glad this worked out," she said.

"All I know is I feel like I can only trust two people, and I can't believe Seton's one of 'em," I said.

Seton cleared his throat. "All my debts are resolved?"

I nodded. "We're straight."

"Okay, then fuck you on your shitty remark. There'll be no more free legal advice."

"And there'll be no more loans to support your gambling," I said. "Your guaranteed pay-offs aren't very guaranteed, asshole."

Jess walked to the kitchen, opened the fridge, and got out the package of chicken. She smiled as she opened a drawer and got a knife. When she got a plate out of the cupboard, I realized she had been in my home enough that she knew where everything was, and I found an odd comfort in knowing that she did.

I had never allowed anyone to grow as close to me as Jess, and seeing her prepare the leopard's food made me view her in a more maternal sense. I shook it off as being a sleep deprived state-of-mind that I would not have possessed otherwise.

"Seton," I said. "I'm taking the diamond to the safe, and I'm going to grab you $100,000 for your quick thinking on this deal. Don't gamble it away."

"Damn. I wasn't expecting that," he said.

"And after I give it to you, you're going to leave. I'm tired, and I'm ready for bed."

"What about me?" Jess asked.

I turned around. "You? You're staying. We're going to have some celebratory sex."

"I just have to stay off my knees," she said. "They're still pretty banged up."

"Duly noted," I said with a laugh.

My sexual interest in Jess had changed so much since we met. I went from wanting to shove her full of dick just to claim her as another notch on my belt to wanting to have sex with her because I cared for her deeply.

I couldn't pinpoint the moment things changed, but I really didn't feel the need to. It simply seemed when she found out what I was involved in that she accepted not only my chosen profession, but me. Immediately following, things within me began to change.

I walked to the safe, placed the diamond inside, and grabbed ten $10,000 stacks of the drug money.

Halfway to the door, I stopped.

I turned around, returned the drug money to the safe, and grabbed ten stacks of $10,000 in *clean* money.

I locked the safe, walked to the door, and looked around the room.

Something in me *had* changed.

# TWENTY-SEVEN

## JESS

**WE** rolled around on the bed naked, wrapped in each other's arms. The mood was different. We were kissing and playing around like high school kids. It was nice. For the first time since we started having sex, I was sober; so it may have been the lack of alcohol that brought on the change, but I really doubted it. Something, I was sure, had changed.

I couldn't decide if the change was within me, in Dick, or of was a little of both.

Whatever the case, I liked it.

A lot.

He pinned me on my back, kissed along my upper arm, and eventually reached my neck. Goosebumps rose along my legs while he kissed up my neck until his mouth was against my ear.

I felt his cock pressing the inside of my thigh.

Strangely, I didn't want it.

At least not in me.

Not yet.

I reached down and gripped it loosely in my hand and began to stroke it until it was firm. With his naked body pressed against mine, I felt like we were preparing to make love. Making love was something I wasn't sure that I'd ever really done, and I had mentally set it aside as something that might happen when I was married, and not before.

Most of my sexual escapades had been while drunk, and never lasted for any length of time – generally until I had an orgasm or two – and not any longer.

I closed my eyes and relaxed while he continued to kiss and caress me. I felt special. I felt wanted.

I was filled with emotion.

His body seemed to fit against mine like it belonged in the place he had chosen to lay. His hip was against mine, his chest on my shoulder, and his leg bent at the knee, resting on my thigh. I felt comfortable, and had no desire to move in an effort to get comfortable.

I *was* comfortable.

I allowed myself to get lost in what I was feeling.

I continued to softly stroke his cock, but he seemed to care not. His hand massaged my breasts while he continued to kiss from my neck to my jaw.

"I want to suck your cock so bad, but my knees--" I whispered.

He lifted his head.

I opened my eyes. Instantly, I was lost. He wasn't the asshole I met in the alley. He wasn't the criminal who masterminded the diamond heist. He was a man that I had fallen in love with, and at that moment, I realized I wouldn't settle for anything short of admitting that I loved him.

*I love you.*

His mouth met mine. We embraced in a kiss. As many times as we had fucked before that night, we had never kissed, and I had no real idea what I was missing until his tongue began to lightly dance with mine.

Chills ran along my spine.

I began to rub my hands all over his naked body, searching for the perfect place to grab, to hold, to grip, only to realize there was no perfect spot, only the perfect man.

And he was mine.

At least for the moment.

The kiss satisfied me as completely as anything I had ever experienced. My hands eventually came to rest, my fingertips pressed into the muscular flesh of his back. His hands held my face lightly as we continued with the kiss until we could kiss no more.

He gazed into my eyes.

I tingled from head-to-toe.

Without explanation or any spoken word, he lifted himself from me, turned, and positioned himself beside me with his head close to my thighs and his hips beside my shoulder. Flat on my back, I stared up at the ceiling and wondered.

Mentally ill-prepared for the emotion and euphoria I was feeling, I gulped a choppy breath. I wanted to speak, to say something, to tell him how I felt, how he made me feel, and how deeply I enjoyed what we were doing.

But I was afraid.

I didn't want to change anything.

I opted to keep my mouth shut, and for some reason, he did too. Maybe, I guessed, he felt no differently than I did, and didn't want it to end.

He lifted his hips and began to climb on top of me, lifting his cock above my face. I craned my neck and encompassed the head of his dick in my mouth, lightly sucking against the soft flesh as he lowered himself onto me.

A jolt ran through me as his tongue flicked against my clit.

*Oh. My. God.*

The thought of sucking his cock while he licked my pussy was beyond exciting. I imagined it being a contest, each of us attempting to either match the other's oral sexual performance or exceed it, and all of it would happen in unison.

Like synchronized swimmers, executing each movement perfectly in time with each other.

I eagerly took him into my mouth.

He slid a finger into my wetness.

I began to work my mouth up and down the shaft while his hips began to softly buck in perfect time with my movements.

His finger worked in and out of my wet slit, and at the same time, his mouth kissed and sucked my swollen nub. I raised my ass from the bed and pressed my pussy against his mouth.

A tingling sensation ran from my nipples to my clit, and returned – repeatedly.

He inserted another finger. In response, I took more of him into my mouth.

He began to moan. The pace of his thrusts increased slightly, ever so gently forcing more and more cock into my mouth. Having the tip deep in my throat turned me on terribly, and I, too, began to moan against the flesh of his swollen shaft.

I felt a fingertip against my asshole. In anticipation of him entering me, I began to suck his cock wildly. He pushed his fingers deep within my pussy and curled the tips of them against my g-spot.

Something I had tried to find with little luck, he had found without instruction.

His fingertips tickled the sensitive flesh, sending a wave of ecstasy through me. I reached up, gripped his tight ass in my hands, and forced his cock deep into my throat.

His finger penetrated my ass.

*Dear God.*

He sucked and licked my clit while his fingers fucked my ass and pussy at the same time. In and out his fingers worked me into a puddle of emotion while he nibbled and sucked my love button with precision.

I felt myself quickly racing to climax.

I thrust my hips up from the mattress over and over, fucking against his face. The sound of him sucking my pussy alone was enough to bring me to orgasm, but his fingers made it so much more enjoyable.

My body shuddered in orgasm and I groaned against his cock, burying it deep in my throat. I needed a breath of air desperately, but at that moment I would have rather died than stopped short of satisfying him.

Another orgasm shot through me deeply, causing my muscles to contract. I pulled down on his ass, forcing the last inch of his manhood into my mouth.

He let out a groan, his hips made two or three short thrusts, and his warmth filled my throat.

Eagerly, I swallowed him completely, satisfied that I had pleased him.

I relaxed into the mattress. He rolled to the side. A soft moan escaped his lungs.

And, side-by-side, we fell asleep.

\*\*\*

The feeling of being kissed washed over me and I felt a heavy weight pressing down on me.

I opened my eyes.

Dick was on top of me, and the room was lit only by the little bit of moonlight that shone in through the windows. I returned the kiss eagerly, desiring more. I wanted what we had before, earlier in the night.

Soon, I got exactly what I wished for.

After the passing of another magical moment, I was lost in a state of bliss. I continued to kiss him, grateful he was able to make me feel so special with nothing more than a simple kiss.

His hand fumbled between us. I felt pressure against my throbbing pussy.

*Oh fuck.*

My eyes went wide as his length slowly pushed into me fully. Being stuffed with ten inches of cock all at once was a feeling in itself, and I never wanted the experience of the first thrust to end.

The kissing continued and the fucking began.

Our mouths parted.

Between his thrusts, I expressed my satisfaction. "Your. Cock. Feels so. Good."

"It's your tight pussy," he assured me.

I wrapped my arms around him and held him tight as he fucked me deeply. I wanted to feel his body against mine, smell his scent, feel his skin, and listen to him breathe. I got all of that, and more, one thrust at a time.

My hands worked my way up and down his body until they came to rest against the cheeks of his ass.

With his muscular butt in my grip, I became the driving force behind his thrusts. Pulling against his flesh, I timed them perfectly, hiking my feet high into the air and spreading my legs as wide as I was able.

I wanted all of him that he was able to give.

His balls slapped against the sensitive skin between my butt cheeks, driving me wild in anticipation of each penetration. I wrapped my legs over his shoulders, and relished in the sight of the shadows the moonlight created along his muscular silhouette.

I wanted him in my ass, but didn't dare ask. I was sober, and I didn't want him to think lesser of me.

He reached beside the bed as he continued to fuck me, seeming to be fumbling for something. In a few seconds, I felt his hand along my thigh, and then a cold wet substance on my ass.

*Oh God.*

*Please.*

He slowly withdrew his cock from inside me.

He stroked his cock with the lube, driving me insane with anticipation. His finger first, and after a few preparatory strokes, his cock pressed into me slowly.

I closed my eyes.

I needed nothing but a few strokes to satisfy me completely.

What he gave me was so much more.

He pushed each of his thumbs into my pussy, and his cock deep into my ass. With his hands, he thumb-fucked me, the web of his hands pummeling my clit with each stroke of his digits.

At the same time, he fucked my ass like it was the last time he was going to have a chance.

I would have guessed ten inches of cock deep in my ass would have killed me, but it was nothing short of perfect. I focused on the shadows cast on his perfect physique, alternating to his handsome face as he fucked my ass like a man possessed.

I have no idea how much time passed, but whatever the length, I was in ecstasy the entire time.

My clit began to tingle. What felt like an electric shock danced between my pussy and my ass with each stroke of his manhood.

My satisfaction came to a head, and I felt myself begin to explode. "I'm going to come. Hard."

I closed my eyes tight and tried to focus on the feeling of his cock deep in my ass, but instead found myself incapable of focusing on anything but my love for Dick.

Everything slipped away from my mental grasp.

My muscles tensed, loosened, and tensed again. Confused, I opened my eyes.

His back arched, and his breathing became choppy. I watched the muscles in his chest and arms become tense.

The warmth of his cum filled me, and as soon as I felt it within me, I burst out in an orgasm of my own, crying out into the silent room for nothing more than to provide him with an assurance that he was wholly and completely the man of my dreams.

His upper body came to rest on my chest, and once again our lips pressed to one another. Passionately, we kissed for some time.

When he pulled his mouth from mine, I returned his passionate look, wanting to say something to give what we shared a label, recognition, something…

"Jess, I love you," he said.

My lip began to quiver. I raised my index finger, knowing an immediate response was impossible. Tears were welling in my eyes and I was busy processing what he had said. A tear rolled down my cheek.

The moment I had waited a lifetime for was well upon me. My lips parted. "I love you, too. But please, be gentle with my heart."

"I will," he assured me with a nod. "Because you're all I have."

And I began to softly cry.

# TWENTY-EIGHT

## DICK

**JESS** and I sat on my back deck enjoying the sun and eating lunch. Seton was on his way over, and I was anxious to learn what he had found out regarding the people I assumed were business associates, but was afraid had all turned snitch.

After hearing his car in the drive, I sent him a text message.

***Come around through the yard. Leopard hates men.***

I chuckled a laugh at the thought of the leopard warming up to Jess and not allowing me within twenty feet of it.

"What?" Jess asked.

"Your cat," I said.

"She loves me."

I shook my head. "Hates me."

Seton came around the corner of the house. "Lunch in the sun?"

Jess raised her half-eaten sandwich. "Hungry?"

"Just ate, thank you."

Anxious, I turned toward him. "So, what'd you learn."

"A considerable amount, actually. Some of which I know, some I've assumed."

"Tell me what you know."

He removed a folded sheet of paper from his jacket. "Well, Drake

Allen Shuck was detained, questioned, and scared shitless to the point that he turned confidential informant on a state level. Bartholomew Bright, no middle initial or name, was charged with possession of stolen diamonds, and he turned confidential informant for the federal government. Bartholomew, in an effort to minimize his exposure to prison time, set up William James Patterson, aka Fat Willie, up on a reverse sting."

"Holy crap, I knew that fat fuck was a cop," Jess said excitedly.

Seton nodded. "Well, he is."

"I can't believe this shit; my entire support system has gone snitch. So, who busted me in the head and took the diamond?" I asked.

"Well, based on what I know, this is what seems to have happened," Seton said. "Your jeweler is on the up and up from what I can see. It seems somehow, by happenstance or because he simply followed you, Duc took your diamond at the jeweler's. He then met with Drake regarding the stone, which was made a matter of record in Drake's case. Drake then set Duc up on a sale to the feds, which was their hope and intention the entire time. They were after him, and didn't want to get him on the purchase, but the sale of the stone. The courts prefer to prosecute sales over purchases. A bargain purchase is often lost in court due to either entrapment or the deal simply being so good it lures the otherwise law-abiding citizen to break the law. Sales, on the other hand are a slam dunk."

"So Duc smacked me, took the stone, and then what?" I asked.

"Duc Nguyen sold it to the federal agents. This I know. So, it stands to reason he is the one who smacked you. At any rate, the feds went to your jeweler, and said if anyone came around asking about buying said stone – or anything of the kind – to give them a call. They not only went to your jeweler; they went to all jewelers who deal with diamonds on a large scale."

"Interesting."

"So, why bust Jess? A law-abiding woman?"

"Well, here's the thing with the feds. They couldn't give a shit who they bust or how. All they want is a statistic. And, feds don't play by any rules, so when they went to the jewelers. They had the man with the mustache – Special Agent Whitmire – act as a man who had a stone for sale. They didn't make it known that they were federal agents. It's not uncommon. They're a shitty bunch to deal with."

"So she was just a fall guy? Or fall girl in this instance?"

He folded the paper and put it back in his pocket. "That is correct."

"Those fuckers."

"Another tidbit for you. The Ferrari's VIN was checked when it was parked, probably while you were in the bar, and it came up as stolen. They opted to wait and see if it was going to be used in the heist. When you pulled in front of the bar, they were certain you were the actual buyer. They had hopes of busting you, but they didn't know who *you* were, as the car is not registered to you. When you slipped away, you became somewhat of a ghost. They questioned the previous owner of the car, and he said nothing. Seems he was scared."

"My favorite car is stolen?" Jess screeched.

"Long story," I said.

She chuckled. "No wonder they were chasing us."

"He should be scared," I said. "Fucker owes me three hundred k."

Seton alternated glances between us. "I'm just glad it's over."

"Well, I'll be damned," I said. "So, mystery solved. But, I've got to find another fence, more buyers, and, well, everyone. This will make my job a little tougher."

"I've got to get," Seton said. "Headed out to Vegas tonight."

"Don't you dare gamble that money away, you idiot," I warned.

He stood up. "I've got a win coming, I can feel it."

"Bye Seton," Jess said with a wave.

"See ya, kid."

I nodded. "Seton."

"See ya, Dick."

"So what now?" Jess asked.

"Well, I said. I've got a diamond to sell. And it looks like I need to find a new crew. Fuck, who can you trust? That's what I want to know. Who the fuck can I trust?"

Jess shrugged. "Nobody but me and Seton."

"Isn't that the truth," I agreed.

And I knew, deep down inside, that she was right.

\*\*\*

"What's the zero to sixty time?" I asked.

The salesman shrugged. "I'm not sure."

"What do you mean you're not fucking sure? It's published somewhere, isn't it? It's performance data. This is a performance car, right?"

"Yes, it is."

"Well?"

"I don't know that we provide those numbers. It promotes speeding and street racing."

I shook my head in sheer disgust. "It promotes sales. The car has almost five hundred horsepower. It weights three thousand pounds. What the fuck else is someone going to do with it?"

He shoved his hands into his pants pockets, pursed his lips, and shrugged.

The political correctness of society aggravated me.

"Get the keys to this little fucker, I want to drive it."

"Let me get them," he said.

I opened the door and looked inside while he was walking away. The red leather interior was a great compliment to the white exterior. Similar to the Ferrari, it had paddle shifters and no clutch pedal. My guess was that it would be pretty fun to drive.

I realized I loved Jess, and I wanted her to know how I felt about her. Buying her flowers, a card, or some other dumb shit just seemed stupid. She had a shitty car, a crappy job, and only $50 extra bucks a week, so devised a little plan to resolve her woes and help me at the same time. The first part of the plan involved getting her a car.

The way she enjoyed the day we ran from the cops told me a performance model would make her happier than anything else.

"Here you go." He pressed the button, unlocked the doors, and handed me the keys.

I opened the door. He did the same. "I don't need a chauffeur," I said.

"Policy."

I started the car, listened to the drone of the exhaust, and grinned. It sounded healthy. We both secured our seatbelts and I pulled out of the lot and onto the street.

"If you take this back to 183, you can go down to…"

"I'm not going to 183, I'm going to go up McNeil to Parmer," I said.

He scowled. "We have a preferred route."

"Are you fucking kidding me? A preferred route? I'm the one buying this motherfucker, I'll drive it where the fuck I want."

He pulled his cell phone from his pocket and made a call. "We're taking an alternate route. McNeil to Parmer."

"What the fuck? You had to call that in?"

He shrugged. "It's policy."

I pulled up to the traffic light and stopped as it switched to yellow. A new Dodge Challenger R/T pulled to the light beside me. Unlike the BMW M4, the Dodge's exhaust rumbled, the car shook, and it was obviously a performance car.

I glanced at the driver of the Dodge. He met my gaze. I nodded toward the light. He nodded in response.

"Don't you dare…"

The light turned green, and I stomped the gas.

The car lunged forward and the engine revved, leaving the Dodge a few feet behind. The tachometer quickly rose to the 7,500 rpm redline, and I tapped the paddle shifter.

The Dodge slowly crept to my side.

Once again, the redline, and another quick shift.

The salesman screamed like a little girl as the BMW climbed to 100 miles an hour. "You can't do this…"

"Shut up. I *am* doing it."

The redline again, another gear, and we shot onto the highway at 125 miles an hour. The Dodge was twenty feet behind us.

I maneuvered around the 70 mile-an-hour traffic, swerving in and out of lanes. The car quickly reached 155 miles an hour, at which point it stopped increasing speed like it had hit a brick wall.

I looked in the rearview mirror. The Dodge was nowhere in sight. "What the fuck? This thing hit a wall at 155?"

He fought to catch his breath as I slowed down to 80. "The U.S. models are electronically limited."

"Can you remove it?" I asked.

He inhaled a deep breath. "What?"

"The fucking limiter?"

"We can, but it'll cost you."

"The girl I'm buying this for will want it removed. If you can remove it, I'll take it."

He coughed out a laugh. "This car isn't a car for a *girl*."

"Well. This isn't a typical girl," I said.

"She better not be," he said. "Not with *this*."

"She's not," I assured him. "Not even close."

# TWENTY-NINE

## JESS

**"WHERE** are we going?" I asked.

"I already told you. Lunch," Dick responded.

"Why are we driving the family car? And where for lunch?"

"It's not a family car, it's a performance sedan. And I don't know yet."

"It has four doors. That's two too many," I said. "And, I want that noodle soup."

He changed lanes, passed a slow-moving truck, and glared at me. "I like this car."

"It's a sedan. I don't like sedans."

He pulled against the paddle shifter three times and mashed the gas.

The car took off like a rocket. In a few seconds we were going twice the speed of the traffic. "Holy shit!" I shouted.

"See?"

"Okay," I admitted. "It's a performance sedan. But it's still a sedan."

He exited the highway and pulled up to the stop light beside the BMW dealership.

I pointed toward the display of cars. "See? They have a ton of BMWs that are coupes."

"Let's have a look," he said.

He turned into the lot and parked. A salesman came running up to the car and asked if he wanted to trade it in on a new M5.

"It is new," Dick said.

We laughed and eventually walked in to the showroom. A white car sat on the showroom floor with a big red bow tied around the top of it.

"Awwe. That's so cute," I said.

"What?" he asked.

"The car with the bow."

"What?" he asked. "You like the bow?"

"Yeah, but look at the car. It's different than the rest of the coupes. See how it sits lower, and has the performance wheels? It's got a mean look to it. It looks fast."

I liked that I knew a little bit about cars, and I wasn't a typical girl when it came to vehicles. If I was rich, I would have a car like the white car and I would drive it fast everywhere I went.

My car, on the other hand, was a piece of shit. It wasn't even paid for, and I had a payday loan against it in addition to the bank loan.

Dick walked around to the back of the car and looked at the trunk. "It's an M4," he said. "It *is* the performance model."

"Told ya," I said.

"Look at the top. It's a convertible."

I laughed. "It is not, it's a hardtop."

"No, actually the BMWs have a hard top," he said. "But it retracts into the trunk. Best of both worlds."

He walked around to the side. Out of curiosity, I asked the price. He glanced at the window sticker. "This one's 91 grand with the options it has."

"Holy crap," I said. "Let's go eat."

It really didn't matter if it was 90 dollars or ninety grand, I couldn't afford it. As I mentally prepared to leave, a salesman walked up to us and shook Dick's hand.

"Dick, right? I remember you when you bought the blue M5."

"Yep. Good memory," Dick said. "Hey can you answer a question?"

"Sure."

"Why's this got a bow on it?"

"Well, it's been sold. Someone bought it as a gift for a special person."

*Some rich fucker.*

"We're waiting for her to pick it up," he said.

*Awwe, it's a her. He bought it for his wife.*

"Huh. What's her name? The lucky girl?"

"Jessica." The salesman said.

My heart skipped a beat. I knew the car wasn't for me, but it was really cool to think about the person who was getting it had my same name.

"Jessica? No shit?" Dick said. "Jessica what?"

"Shunk," the salesman said.

My legs did the wobbly thing. I raised my hand like a kindergartner wanting to ask a question of the teacher. "Huh? Who?"

"Shunk," he said. "Jessica Shunk."

My hands were shaking. I looked at Dick. Dick shrugged. I looked at the salesman. He grinned.

"My name's Jessica Shunk."

"You don't say," he said. "Do you have an I.D.?"

I nodded. "But it's got to be a coincidence."

"Well, do you know your driver's license number? We have it saved

223

for her under her driver's license number."

I reached into my purse, pulled out my wallet, and stared down at my license. "TS-901-497--"

"7557?" he asked.

I bit my lower lip and nodded my head. I felt faint. It couldn't be. There was no way…

"I love you, Jess," Dick said.

I looked at the salesman. He nodded and smiled. I looked at Dick. He grinned. It made no sense that they'd play with someone's emotions the way they were. I actually thought it was true.

"Well." Dick reached into his pocket. "Here's the key."

*You're serious?*

I swallowed hard. "You're serious."

He tossed me the key.

I pressed the button on the key fob. The lights flashed. I pressed it again. They flashed again.

"Dick?"

He walked around the edge of the car and gave me a kiss. "I love you. Enjoy it."

My eyes welled with tears. "It's really…"

"It sure is."

"Dick it's…"

"It's yours. It's already paid for, so no arguing."

He must have sold the diamond. I shook my head. "I love you too."

"You're driving to lunch," he said. "Let's go."

I looked around. We were surrounded by glass. "How do we get out of here."

"If you want to take the bow off, I'll open up the south wall," the salesman said.

My heart was racing. I helped Dick remove the bow, put it in the trunk, and got inside. After a quick adjustment of the seat, I gripped the steering wheel and looked around the interior.

"It's just like the Ferrari. Double clutch manual with no pedal. Just paddle shifters."

"Holy shit!" I said. "That's awesome. Dick, it's perfect."

"Where are we going for lunch?" he asked.

"I've got an idea," I said.

"Where?" he asked.

"You'll see."

# THIRTY

# DICK

"Where are we going for lunch?" I asked in as whiny of a voice as I could.

With her sunglasses on and the top down, Jess paid little attention to my question. She signaled and changed lanes. A few seconds later, she signaled and changed back.

"Where are we going for lunch?"

"You'll see," she said.

I suspected we were going to the soup kitchen. She'd been asking about it for some time, and was upset that she didn't get to finish her bowl of soup on the night we saw Drake and Duc.

"Soup?" I asked.

With the top down, the wind blew her hair in every direction. She tapped her fingers against the steering wheel. "Nope."

It was rewarding seeing her pleased with the car. It was the least I could do for her, considering how much she meant to me. I had much more planned for her, but had to wait until we were somewhere we could talk before I could go into detail.

She got off the highway, pulled up to the stoplight, and turned on the turn signal.

"We going shopping?" I asked.

227

"Nope."

The left arrow turned green and she sped through the light. Another lane change. this time to the right, and she pulled into Target.

"Remember this place?" she asked.

I nodded. "How could I forget?"

"You're going to fuck me with the top down."

I laughed. "We'll get arrested."

"Not if you're careful."

"And quick," I said.

She pulled in behind the store, almost in the same spot I had parked in previously. Out of the way of traffic, but still in clear view for the perverts and rubberneckers to see, she parked.

"I'm going to fuck you senseless," she said.

"Hey, that's my line."

There had been so many changes in my life in the last few months, none of which I regretted. Not one of them was easy to believe, but they were easy for me to accept. I would never second guess Jess' existence in my life – she was perfect for me, and the only answer to resolving my otherwise dismal love life.

"Take off your pants," she demanded.

"Such a romantic."

I glanced over each shoulder and upon seeing no one, unbuckled my belt. She lasted all of fifteen seconds before deciding to help me pull them down. As soon as they were at my thighs, she removed her jean shorts and tossed them in the back seat. Panties followed.

She stroked my cock a few times, but I was well beyond excited as it was. Standing at complete attention, my cock was pointing at the sky. Sitting in the driver's seat, she spread her legs a little, stuck her finger in her pussy, and grinned.

"Soaked," she said. "Always wet for you."

"Good."

She climbed over the console and straddled me with her back against my chest. As I felt her wetness touch the tip of my dick, I moaned in anticipation. She exhaled sharply as her tight warmth encompassed the tip. I watched as she slowly lowered herself down the entire length, resting her ass against my thighs once I was completely inside of her.

"Ready?" she asked.

I laughed at her sense of humor. "I love you."

She slapped her hands against the dash and began to work her hips back and forth with precision. I watched in amazement as my cock disappeared into her pussy only to be withdrawn with another gyration of her beautiful ass.

I reached around her and squeezed her breasts, using them as leverage to guide her up and down.

The warm sun, the passing cars, and the thought of being back at the Target where we had sex after I lost the diamond – but didn't yet trust her enough to tell her what happened – proved to be too much.

"I'm not going to make it," I admitted.

She glanced over her shoulder. "Are you gonna cum?"

"Yeah…" I groaned.

She stuck her hand between her legs and began to rub her clit.

I felt my balls tighten.

"Wait for me," she begged.

I bit against my lower lip and did my best to think of anything that would allow me to last a few more seconds. She continued the same pace, banging her ass down on my thighs, taking my cock into her completely with each thrust.

Watching myself disappear into her tight pussy was more than I could take. My cock began to swell.

"Fuck yes," she wailed.

Her ass continued to rise and fall, but her pace slowed slightly. I felt her contract. I squeezed her boobs as I felt myself burst inside of her, pumping her full of my love.

"I fucking love you," I breathed into her ear.

She thrust her hips three more times, barking out a word with each thrust.

"I..."

"Love..."

"You..."

She sat still for some time, absorbing all of what had happened. A good few minutes after we finished, she sighed and looked over her shoulder. "I love my car."

I glanced around. Cars passed on either side of us, but where we were parked wasn't a through traffic way. "I'm glad. I hoped you would."

"I'm gonna get off now," she said.

I grinned. "I'm ready."

She climbed off of me, and cum flopped out of her and all over my jeans.

"Don't get that shit on my car," she howled.

I looked down at the puddle of cum. "What do you want me to do?"

She shrugged as she pulled her shorts on. "Rub it into your jeans."

Reluctantly, I followed her instructions. After we were both dressed, I turned to face her.

"So, I told you the car was part of it. Now that we've got time to talk,

I have a few questions."

"Okay," she said.

"Well, I don't do cheesy shit, and I'm not much of a romantic, but I'll do my best," I said.

She grinned. "I'm listening."

"You know I love you. More than anyone, more than anything, right?"

She nodded. "I do."

"Jess, my life wasn't a disaster, and I'm not going to tell you it was. I wasn't lost. I didn't need saved. Neither did you. I don't know if you were, but I wasn't looking when I found you. Life just kind of happened. Along with it came love. I wasn't prepared, but I guess I was ready, because it all worked out. Now? Now that I've had you in my life? I can't imagine anything but keeping you. Forever."

I reached into my pocket and removed the ring.

I held it up for her to see. Completely custom made with 4 carats of side stones and *the* 10 carat center stone, the ring was beyond breathtaking. I shifted my eyes from the ring to Jess.

Her mouth was covered with her hand and her eyes were glued to the ring.

I cleared my throat. "Will you be my partner? My partner in life, my partner in love, and my partner in crime."

In my former life, I would have never considered keeping the diamond. The $3,500,000 in proceeds from the ring would allow me to continue my life of robbing from the assholes on the earth and providing to those in need.

But if she would agree to be my partner, I knew deep down inside we could make the money back without worry.

Jess was an amazing woman, and an amazing criminal mastermind. I couldn't imagine a life without her, and I couldn't fathom continuing my life of crime if the only person on earth I was able to trust wasn't in it with me.

She wiped a tear from her cheek and nodded. "I will."

I slipped the ring on her finger and kissed her passionately.

As our mouths parted, I felt I should say something, but as much as I wanted to, I was so deeply in love with her, I was speechless.

We sat silently and stared into each other's eyes.

We didn't have to speak, our love for each other said it all.

A wise woman once said *love is when your heart has feelings for a person that your mind is incapable of putting into words.*

And she was right.

# EPILOGUE

"**WHO** is this guy again?" I asked as I carefully placed the jewelry Dick had set aside into a foam padded case.

"He was a hedge fund manager that took people's money in 2007 and 2008, and was never convicted," Dick said as he stuffed cash and other paperwork into a canvas bag.

"How much total?" I asked.

"How much are we taking, or how much did he swindle people for?"

"Both," I said.

"Roughly $2,000,000 tonight." He glanced at his watch. "And he fucked people out of almost $20,000,000, but got off scot-free. Come on, we're down to two minutes."

Even though we circumvented the alarm system, Dick didn't like to be in a house for longer than five minutes. I didn't disagree.

"I've got all the jewelry," I said.

"Just about done," he said.

I walked to the stairway and waited while he finished loading the contents of the safe. On the wall hung a picture of a boy, probably a senior picture from high school.

He looked eerily like Dick.

"How did you know exactly where the safe was?" I asked as I studied the photo.

"Truth or a lie?" he asked.

"Tell me a lie," I said.

"Blind luck," he responded.

"Dick," I said.

"Yeah, Baby?"

"Are we robbing your parent's house tonight?"

"We sure are, Baby."

"Dick!"

"He's one rotten motherfucker, Baby."

"Okay, you're the boss."

He ran to my side, hoisted the bag over his shoulder, and looked down the stairs. "Ready?"

I nodded. "Always and forever."

\*\*\*

Dressed in shorts, hiking boots, and an orange tank top, I walked into the Lowe's hardware store and to the *returns* counter.

A pale tattooed girl with purple hair walked up the counter. "What can I help you with?"

"Can you tell me which department Raymond Gonzalez works in?"

Her mouth shot into a smile. "Ray? Yeah, he's in electronics. You won't be able to miss him."

I turned around, paused, and glanced over my shoulder. "Why do you say that?"

"He'll be the one telling someone a story. To whoever listens."

I grinned at her response and walked along the main aisle toward the sign suspended from the ceiling that said *electronics*.

When I reached the sign, I turned to the right. A middle-aged

Hispanic man stood twenty feet away telling two young employees a tale. I faked interest in a row of wall receptacles and waited for him to finish. After a few minutes, he excused himself from the conversation, explaining to the workers that he needed to help me.

"Is there something in particular you're looking for?"

According to the paperwork Dick got in the robbery from his father's home, Mr. Gonzalez lost his entire retirement – close to $400,000. Depending on how he would have invested it, it may have accrued another $150,000 in interest – or more – over the last 8 years.

His nametag said Ray. I asked anyway. "Raymond Gonzalez?"

He looked like any other middle-aged Hispanic man. He was tan, had black hair that was starting to turn gray, and inviting brown eyes. With a nod and a cheery smile, he responded. "I'm Ray."

I glanced over each shoulder and after seeing no one, pulled the pack off my shoulders.

"I'm going to make this quick, and them I'm going to go."

He returned a worried look. "Okay."

"You lost roughly $400,000 in 2008? Your entire retirement plan?"

He nodded, and along with the acknowledgement, came a rush of emotion. Before I was able to say another word, he was overcome, and his lip began to quiver.

"I uhhm...I...Yeah. I...uhhm."

"I'm sorry it happened to you, but it's all gonna get better when you take this bag." I glanced over my shoulders again. "There are two gold bars in it, and each one is worth roughly $500,000. It's my gift to you."

He looked like he wanted to trust me, but I fully understood his reluctance. "Who are you?"

I wanted to tell him about Dick, and how we robbed rich assholes and drug dealers and gave the money to people who we felt needed it. But. I knew I couldn't, so I simply offered a shrug and the response that I had learned was best.

"Just some girl." I said.

He unzipped the bag and peered inside. His eyes met mine and went wide.

I nodded and fought not to cry.

"I can take this?"

"You can."

"You have no idea…" He paused, incapable of continuing.

A tear rolled down his cheek.

I waved and turned around.

As I walked to the parking lot, a tear escaped my eye.

I got in the car, turned toward Dick, and wiped the tears from my face. "You were right."

"How so?"

"It feels so good," I said. "And the look on his face? I just…"

"Good shit, huh?"

I nodded and fought against the tears. "I love you."

"Love you, Baby."

I shifted the car into reverse and paused for a moment. I knew my life would never be the same. I'd always be looking over my shoulder and living in a manner that wouldn't allow me many true friends. I had Dick in my life, and I didn't need anyone else. The risk was too high.

And I wasn't in the risk taking business.

I was a criminal and an asshole.

And I was good at being both.

www.ingramcontent.com/pod-product-compliance
Lightning Source LLC
Chambersburg PA
CBHW050738180626
46814CB00002B/811